Shadowfall

A Novel of Sherlock Holmes

Tracy Revels

Paperback ISBN 9781908218254
Mobipocket/Kindle ISBN 9781908218261
ePub ISBN 9781908218278

Published in the UK by MX Publishing
335 Princess Park Manor, Royal Drive, London, N11 3GX
www.mxpublishing.co.uk

Cover artwork by www.staunch.com

To The Survivors of the Gloria Scott

The story I am about to tell must never be told.

If you are reading these words in some time and place far from my own, years and miles removed from the quiet domesticity of an English home in the late nineteenth century, then you will no doubt consider me a madman. You will reflect, you unknown reader who considers these scrawled line not by gaslight or electricity, but by some illumination as yet unknown to science, that Dr. John H. Watson was either a harmless eccentric or a dangerous lunatic. You will think yourself fortunate to have never known him or been forced to listen to his insane prattling. You will mock him, and perhaps invite others to laugh at his poor addled brain, which somehow conjured these disturbing images.

But I tell you they are true.

And yet they must never be known.

For many years I was the boon companion to the wisest man the world had ever seen, a man renowned for his skills in detection and famed for bringing the foulest villains to justice, even at great peril to his own life. He was a man who battled the demons of the criminal underworld, who conquered societal corruption and moral decay. He was hailed and honoured by crowned heads of Europe; indeed, he was on terms of some intimacy with the Queen herself. Everyone knew his name, his residence, his likeness.

5

And no one knew him at all.

This is the story that must never be told. I confess that I often, without any awareness of the truth, hinted at it in my writings, through a word I placed in the mouths of those who were amazed by his seemingly inhuman powers. But it was the truest word I ever wrote about him, the one that defined him best and the one that he embodied when he saved not only my life, but my very soul.

You may not believe this story, but I must write it down before my memories fade. My confession concerns the true nature of Sherlock Holmes.

Chapter One

It was an April morning in a year late in the century. London was finally rousing itself from a long winter's sleep, and the air was soft, filled with the fragrance of flowers bursting from window boxes. I had some errands to do, and as the weather was unusually balmy I told Holmes---who had barely roused himself to come to the breakfast table and glare at the kippers---that I would not return until the late afternoon. But in truth, it was more than business and the urge for a constitutional around the metropolis that drove me from our rooms at 221 B Baker Street.

Holmes had been in something of a fugue state for several days, answering my inquiries in grunts and snorts, lying around on the sofa and lighting a new cigarette with the remains of the last, until the atmosphere in our rooms was poisonous and intolerable. It was a familiar reaction to me. I was well acquainted with the ennui Holmes fell into when no case of merit presented itself to him, and his brain, like a finely-tuned machine, began grinding gears. At such times, I feared he would return to the cocaine bottle. I had weaned him of that vile habit some years before, but it remained a spectre in our companionship, a fiend lurking in the shadows, ready to spring. If embracing the demons of his addiction was his intention today, I did not wish to witness it. So perhaps it was as much cowardice as impatience driving me from our residence that morning.

I took luncheon in the Strand, spent some time ambling through the shops on Oxford Street, and considered dropping by my club, only to realize that I had insufficient funds should one of the lads challenge me to a game of billiards. Finding myself only a short walk from home, I decided to return and fetch the purse that I kept for just such diversions. Perhaps this would give my friend a chance to test his powers, should he attempt to deduce why I had returned so unexpectedly. My good spirits, buoyed by the beauty of the day, were such that I mentally wagered him a shilling that he could not divine my purpose. It was not, after all, my usual days for billiards.

Thus it was that I flung open the door to our sitting room without preamble or announcement, and found, to my great astonishment, that a naked woman with gossamer wings was sitting on our sofa.

There is a moment between dreaming and waking in which reality seems a thread that can be stretched, twirled and twisted into a thousand different shapes. In this instant, even the most fantastic illusion can be accepted as fact. It was in this netherworld that I seemed suspended, especially as the woman turned and acknowledged my presence with a coquettish laugh.

"So this is the famous Dr. Watson!"

8

"Famous for his inability to knock, I should think," Holmes answered from where he stood beside the fireplace. His voice was thick with annoyance and his eyes had never been colder. I felt myself gasping for air. I stumbled backward, grabbing at the door handle, missing it repeatedly.

"Yes, well....ah...do forgive me. I...I shall...retire."

"Watson, front and centre, man," Holmes barked, with all the authority of a general in the Afghan campaign. "There's no going back now." He extended a hand, gesturing toward the unclad woman. "I present to you Titania, Queen of the Fairies."

My wooden, nerveless legs somehow propelled me forward. The woman seemed not to sit so much as to float above the furnishing, her silky wings keeping her aloft with tiny, trembling flutters. She was as naked as Eve, her body slim and yet beautifully proportioned, her skin warm and rosy. Her long lavender hair waved around her head as if suspended underwater. Her eyes were narrow and sharply angled, directing the viewer's gaze to the razor-points of her ears. Her mouth was sensual, her lips full and flush, but when she spoke I saw that her teeth were filed like some African pygmy's. Each tooth formed a little dagger within her mouth.

I found I could not speak. How does one greet such a sensual illusion?

Sensing my discomfort, she smirked at me and extended a hand. Blindly, I bent and kissed it.

"We are gratified to see that our Sherlock has such a noble and stout-hearted companion," she said, in a voice of tinkling bells. As she spoke, she flicked her tongue, like a lizard considering a tasty morsel. "And you are a rather handsome man as well."

I felt my face grow hot. I stammered my reply. "I....thank you, Madame."

Her smile tightened. "I am addressed as Majesty."

"Oh, I...do forgive me your—"

"It does not matter how she is addressed," Holmes snapped. He grabbed my arm and tugged me away from the woman, dragging me to the fireside. With those few steps I felt like some great elastic band had been released from my chest and I could once more breathe. "The Most High Queen of the Fairies has concluded her business with me," Holmes stated, "and she is now leaving."

Titania arched a thin brow. "Is this your final word? You reject my humble plea so curtly?"

Holmes folded his arms. "It is not my intention to be churlish, dear lady. But you know how I stand on these matters. I am no longer a servant to your world. I have no intention on crossing into the Shadows again."

The woman smiled wickedly. "To refuse me is to court danger."

Holmes's thin lips twitched. "I am comfortable with danger. It is an old and familiar companion in my work."

"For you, perhaps." Titania's head turned. Her amber gaze fell on me. "But for others?"

Holmes moved between us, giving an imperious wave of his hand.

"Titania, I order you away."

She laughed like a child mocking its nurse. "Really, do you think your mere words have bindings? That you, a son of our house, could force me to leave before I am willing to depart? But I will go, because I know you, have known you since the cradle. Such a puzzle will tempt you back across the Shadows." She put tiny fingers to her lips and blew him a kiss. "And there you will find me waiting."

Her wings crashed together around her. In that instant, she was gone in a vapour that smelled of forests and moss and the first unfurled leaves.

"Holmes," I said some minutes later, when I finally located my voice, "have you been conducting chemical experiments? Something that would affect the brain? Please tell me that you have been burning that dreaded devil's foot again!"

He walked to the mantle, removing his clay pipe and a plug of tobacco. "You are not under the influence of any vile chemical, Watson."

"Then what, in the name of all that is Holy, was that? Who was <u>she</u>?"

"Exactly who she claimed to be---Titania, the immortal Queen of the Fairies. Do sit down, Watson, you are looking rather pale."

I collapsed into the basket chair. "Holmes, this is madness. Fairies do not exist."

"How do you know?" he asked, with a short puff.

"What?" I demanded. He shrugged as he spoke.

"You say they do not exist, because you have never seen one before. But is that, in and of itself, proof that they do not exist? Mankind had never seen germs until the invention of the microscope. People believed that the hand of God caused diseases. If I were to tell you that tiny, nearly invisible creatures inside your body produced your ailments, and you were not already a man of science, would you believe me?"

My head was spinning. I kept glancing at the sofa, expecting Titania to reappear. To regain my composure, I forced myself to grab the sides of the chair until its rough texture bit into my palms.

"No, of course not, but...fairies are nonsense, stories for children and foolish people. As bad as tales of banshees and ghosts and—"

"Spectral dogs?" Holmes asked.

I lifted my head, stared at him sternly. "The hound of the Baskervilles was real. A concoction of phosphorus to the jaws gave him the appearance of the supernatural but he was merely a weapon in the hands of a greedy man, and very real."

"True," Holmes conceded, with the first hint of a smile. "But until you had him at your feet, riddled with bullets, you entertained the possibility that he might be something else. A creature of another world. A being of the Shadows."

"Holmes---please make sense," I pleaded. "Are you implying that there is some other reality, some sphere of existence beyond our own?"

The hint of amusement was abruptly banished from his face. "I am indeed, Watson. There is another world, one called the Shadows."

"Impossible."

"Not impossible. It is world filled with darkness, this space between the spaces of our own, sun-governed reality. Monsters of all forms reside there. You say that this place and these things cannot exist, because you are a rational man who sees nothing. But Watson, you use only a bare fraction of your senses. In truth, you see, but you do not observe."

I shook my head roughly. I felt suddenly enervated, exhausted. The room seemed to spin around me.

"Madness, Holmes," I whispered, rising to my feet. I grabbed the mantel for support. "You are speaking in riddles and lunacies."

"Am I?" he asked, in that old sardonic way of his. "You look rather tired, Watson. Perhaps a siesta of sorts would do you good."

My eyelids were heavy. I could barely focus to walk toward the door to my bedchamber. "Indeed, I....I will take you advice."

"Excellent. Thompson would have beaten you at billiards anyway, given your condition."

I had just enough sense to pause at the door to my room and wonder how he had known my intention to go to my club. Then darkness closed around me, shadows swallowed me, and I was grateful.

Chapter Two

I woke and was startled to find dawn rather than twilight illuminating the street outside my window. My jacket and shoes had been removed and my collar was undone, but I had no memory of attending to these details. My head pounded as if Vulcan were within, beating on his anvil. I sat up gingerly, fighting down nausea. For an instant, a ghost of a very strange dream teased my memory, despite the incessant hammering in my head. But it flitted away before I could seize it and make sense of it.

I moved slowly, and after a torturous progress I stood at last before my mirror. The sight that greeted me looked like an illustration from a 'shilling shocker,' a garish tale of horror written to amuse schoolboys. My hair stood on end and my face was a strange shade of greenish-gray. Bluish bruises ringed my eyes and my lips were crusty. Just to touch my skin caused stabbing pains. I considered tumbling back into the bed, yet I knew that I would not be able to fall asleep, lest I take a starring role in my own nightmares.

After a rather painful washing up, during which my hand trembled so violently I could barely hold my shaving razor, I timidly entered our sitting room. Holmes caught sight of my reflection in the coffeepot and turned with a mocking smile.

"Good morning, Watson." He surveyed me up and down, his expression growing ever more amused. "It looks as if Morpheus dropped you on your head, rather than carrying you in his arms throughout the evening."

Mrs. Hudson, who had been setting the table, turned and gave me an appraisal. "Good heavens, Doctor Watson, you are a fright! Are you ill?" she demanded.

"I feel dreadful," I confessed, as I settled in. "But I do not think I am contagious."

"Here, eat something," Mrs. Hudson ordered. "Food will make you better! You need nourishment."

She lifted the silver lid of the serving dish, revealing a hearty course of bangers and mash. My stomach flipped over, and it took all my self-control not to violently expel its contents across the tablecloth.

"No, please---replace the cover," I begged.

Mrs. Hudson banged the lid down, an action that seemed to open a great chasm in my head. She departed with a righteous huff, deeply offended by my rejection of her offering. I begged for coffee. Holmes was kind enough to pour and I sipped my cup delicately, drinking like an ancient invalid. I could feel Holmes' gaze piercing through me.

"Are you certain you are not sick, Old Chap?" Holmes asked, opening his newspaper.

"I think so," I muttered. Holmes rattled a page of the paper, an action that made a battery of guns explode in my head. "But I still feel terrible."

"Is there a logical explanation for this incapacitation?" my companion inquired, in the most baiting of tones. I easily grasped his meaning.

"Holmes, I know what you are hinting at and, no, I did not go out roistering last night."

"Indeed?" He waved a hand, pointing to me blindly from behind the newsprint. "The evidence before me is most suggestive: the bloodshot eyes, the facial pallor, the unsteady hands. What else would a reasonable man conclude?"

For a long moment, I entertained the idea that Holmes was correct. Perhaps I had encountered some of my old army chums and spent the evening reminiscing over my days in Afghanistan with the Fifth Northumberland Fusiliers. But there was no smell of whiskey on my breath and not even the flicker of a memory of a reunion with old comrades. Surely I would recall a few details of such an unexpected and highly pleasurable event.

"I remember nothing."

"A common side effect of overindulgence in spirits," Holmes remarked, with all the sanctimony of a Salvation Army sergeant. "Or so I have been told."

The temptation to reach across the table and punch the man was nearly irresistible. "Holmes," I defended, "I may be intemperate at times, but I have never lost my memory of a celebration, not since—" I felt a blush rise to my face as I recalled a particularly embarrassing weekend from my youth. "Not since I was in medical school! But I have never, as a grown man, been so intoxicated as to lose the memory of an entire evening." I considered Holmes, as he hid behind *The Times*, with my right eye. It was the only one capable of opening. "This affliction is inexplicable to me."

"Hmmm," Holmes said, with another tortuous rattling of the paper, "most mysterious."

Despite my pounding headache, my fighting spirit was aroused. I refused to let Holmes mock me without demanding that he tell me what had occurred. I had begun to suspect that one of his noxious experiments had gone awry. Indeed, I had never forgotten the words of young Stamford, the army dresser who introduced me to Holmes, that this man was capable of administering the latest poison to a colleague, just to scientifically observe its effects.

"Holmes," I said sternly, gritting my teeth against the pain of speaking aloud at a volume above a whisper, "something happened to me last night, and it has no connection to the fruit of the vine. Or to a lady's charms," I quickly added, now seeing the amusement onto his face as he folded the newspaper. "So kindly, if you value my friendship, explain to me why I have woken up feeling like a sailor just returned from shore leave."

He lit a cigarette and blew smoke at the ceiling. "I have not a clue."

"Holmes, that is beneath you, not to mention cruel. I deduce that this is somehow your fault!"

"My fault?" he asked, with an exaggerated gasp.

"Yes. You and your blasted chemicals, your noxious pipe tobacco, your music that would drive even the sanest man to Bedlam—"

"Watson!" He cut me off, giving me an offended scowl. "Why do you think I was here? I do not spend every evening in these lodgings. Perhaps I was out, tending to an investigation, and therefore did not witness your descent into drunken debauchery."

"You have no case at the moment," I protested. At least my mind was clear enough to remember that fact.

"Are you certain that I tell you everything I do?" he countered. Those words were like a sharp spear, thrust deep into my brain. For just an instant, I seemed to remember things. But they were only tissues, shadows, nothing of substance that I could grab hold of. I closed my eyes and breathed deeply.

"Of course not," I whispered. "You are a very secretive person. I still do not know how many abodes you have in London or how many aliases you live under."

Holmes' little flicker of a smile told me that he took my admission as an apology. He pulled a card from the pocket of his dressing gown.

"As it so happens, I do have a case, newly arrived upon our doorstep as you were dragging yourself back into the land of the living." He tossed the card upon the table, just beside my coffee cup. "Honest work is the best cure for your disease, Watson. Can you be ready in ten minutes?"

I lifted the card, blinking until I could read the words scrawled upon it.

Dreadful outrage at Highgate Cemetery. Please, I beg you, be discreet and come at once.

"It's unsigned."

"An astute observation, Watson," Holmes said, favouring me with a smirk. "But I know the handwriting, and a communication from Highgate can mean only one thing. It is from Charon and no other. Come now, into your armour, the battle draws nigh."

Perhaps it was his choice of words that abruptly brought my nocturnal fantasy back into sharp relief. I dropped my cup on the table, spilling coffee across the card that requested Holmes' presence at that great gathering place of the dead.

"Holmes---was there a naked woman here, yesterday?"

"My blushes, Watson."

"I am quite serious!" I countered. "Was there an unclothed, winged woman in this room, seated upon the sofa?"

He considered me with those great grey eyes. For just a moment, I sensed some debate behind them, some uncertainty. And then he gave his head a shake, snubbing out his cigarette as he spoke.

"You have it on my honour, Watson; there was no woman in these rooms yesterday---beyond Mrs. Hudson, of course, if the evidence of unsightly tidiness is to be believed. And it seems most probable to me that she would have been fully clothed while performing her duties."

"But I have the strongest recollection! Holmes, I am certain that I saw a naked woman---a fairy woman---in this very room."

Holmes rose from the table. The look of disgust on his face made it clear that the subject was closed. "Any memory that you have of a nude woman in this chamber was either a wishful dream or a wistful fantasy. I am interested in neither. Now, are you coming with me or not?"

I could do no more than accept his words. I nodded slightly, returned to my room and reminded myself of my own boast, that I was an old campaigner. To prove it I put on my coat and hat and slipped my army revolver into my pocket. Minutes later, as we rode away in a cab, I pondered my own foolish action. Who did I expect to fire upon in Highgate? Anyone there was already beyond the reach of my bullets.

Chapter Three

It was almost ten in the morning when we reached that grim yet fashionable abode of the dead. As our cab crept along the dreary avenue of Swain's Lane, I recalled some of the stories that I had heard concerning this cemetery. It seemed that the dead rarely rested in peace here, especially if they were rich or famous. For example, on one cold and bitter night, the beautiful bride of the artist and poet Dante Rossetti had been perversely drawn from her grave so that unfeeling minions of her husband could retrieve a book of poems he had placed on her final pillow. There was also the public scandal when the Duke of Wellford was unearthed simply to assure the public that he had been dead and buried and a claimant to his fortune was, in fact, a criminal imposter. I wondered if some similar mischief was afoot.

Holmes signalled for our driver to halt at a side gate and paid the man handsomely to remain and wait for us. It occurred to me, as we entered the hallowed ground, that Holmes was unusually taciturn. It was in his nature, when no facts of a case had yet been presented, to engage in some type of homespun philosophy as we travelled to the scene of the crime. I would have expected our journey to evoke musing on the brevity of life and the inevitability of death. Instead, he remained as stony faced as the marble angels that guarded the graves.

"Mr. Holmes---this way if you will."

I confess that the sudden voice from amid the tombstones gave me a start. A tall, cadaverously thin man stepped out from behind an obelisk memorial. He was dressed in the deepest mourning, with a high black hat upon his head and an ebony cravat tied in a large bow beneath his chin. His entire ensemble was in a style that had gone out of fashion when our good Queen was young. He offered a stiff bow, and regarded my friend with bright, piercing blue eyes that seemed an odd contrast to his deathly pallor.

"Mr. Charon, I find you rather unchanged," Holmes said, in the way of greeting. He motioned toward me, and I was aware the man was staring at me with some agitation, twisting his hands and giving small shivers. "This is my friend and colleague Doctor Watson. You may rely upon his discretion as you would my own."

The man coughed harshly, sounding like a consumption patient upon his deathbed. "Are you certain it is wise to involve him in this matter?" he asked, giving me another look of nervous distain.

"I think it would be folly not to," Holmes relied, and my chest puffed a bit at such words of confidence from my friend. "Now tell me, which corpse has gone missing?"

Charon gasped. "But how could you know that a body has been stolen?"

Holmes favoured him with a disgusted glare. "Why else would you, of all people, be seeking my assistance?"

Holmes' curtness surprised me. It was not unusual for my friend to be brusque to the point of rudeness, and he did not tolerate fools gladly. But this sharpness seemed alien to his nature. Nor did Holmes pause to introduce the man to me properly, or give me his rank or occupation. I merely assumed, from his dress and his bearing, that he was the sexton of the cemetery or perhaps an undertaker. Whatever his position, Mr. Charon ducked his head like a dog whose hindquarters had just felt the swift kick of his master's boot.

"Of course, Mr. Holmes. If you will come this way?"

We followed the man on a path that took us past numerous grand tombs and memorials. I noted the resting places of scientists and businessmen, even a few peers of the realm. At last we reached the stately arch of the Egyptian Avenue, that great artefact of a time when our grandfathers had been consumed by a passion for all things Oriental. Holmes put out a hand, halting our progress. His nostrils flared and he sniffed the air like some majestic hound.

"Have any of the regular forces been summoned, Charon?"

"No, of course not. I felt it best not to make this matter public. The potential for scandal is immense."

A line drew between Holmes' dark eyebrows. "You still have not told me whose tomb was desecrated."

"Lady Ariel Whitborne, Mr. Holmes."

The name was a familiar one, at least to those who read pages dedicated to society. The lady had been an American, a young, coffee-skinned Creole beauty from New Orleans, who made a match with Sir James Whitborne, a widower of an old and distinguished line. He had been sixty and she a mere twenty-two when they wed a year before, shocking all of London and enraging the knight's only son, who made such a public fuss that his father disinherited him. The young man decamped to New York to seek his fortune among the robber barons there, but the recent death of Lady Ariel had led to talk of reconciliation between father and son. As the Whitborne holdings were extensive and the family fortune spoken of as one of the largest in the nation, a loving reunion was cynically predicted by the society gossips.

"How long has the lady been deceased?" Holmes asked, as we pushed on to the stately crypts of the Circle of Lebanon.

"Just over a month," Charon answered.

"And the crypt she was placed in was properly secured?"

"A virtual fortress, Mr. Holmes. As you see..."

We had reached our destination. The violence done to the small, house-like structure was immense. The iron bars that guarded the entrance had been pulled down and flung aside, twisted and bent as if made of rubber. Inside, the coffin that had held the mortal remains of the American beauty was smashed into kindling, its satin and velvet linings shredded upon the stone floor.

I heard Holmes make a soft exclamation. He waved for us to stay back. He stepped in among the debris, examining each fragment with great care. I retreated and considered the ground near the tomb, but it was very hard and not a footprint could be found. Nor was there any indication that the culprits had dropped tools, or shreds of paper, or tobacco ashes, or other vital clues. Holmes rose, holding something in his hand.

"One wonders who she hoped to impress in the afterlife."

I marvelled at a diamond necklace drooping from Holmes' fingertips. Even in the dim light of that cold, grey morning, I could tell that it was worth a king's ransom.

"Grave robbers," I muttered. "Foul, vile creatures. Perhaps a servant or the undertakers who laid out the body did this reprehensible deed."

"Watson," Holmes countered, with no little impatience, "if robbery was the motive, why carry off the body and leave such a prize behind? A diamond necklace is far more portable than a corpse."

I confess that I cringed at my own propensity to draw erroneous conclusions. "Body snatchers, then. But I thought the days of the resurrection men had passed."

"As indeed they have, Watson." Holmes exited the crypt and placed the necklace in Charon's skeletal hand. "Besides, who would want a corpse that was over a month old and thus already significantly decayed? Not to mention the difficulty of breaking into this particular tomb. There are many fresher, much more easily obtained bodies."

I recalled the awful stories I had heard during my days as a medical student, of young men who sometimes saw the remains of family members, or former lovers, upon the dissecting table. At least the lady was spared that fate, though her remains were hardly safe from a different type of indignity. "Holmes," I posed, very cautiously, "could they be holding the body for ransom?"

"If so, then we must wait upon a note to Sir James. At least the victim can have no more mortal harm done to her, however shocking the crime."

"And you will leave it there?" Charon demanded, when Holmes turned on his heel and started toward the Egyptian archway. "You can not!"

Holmes swung his cane to his shoulder, answering without looking backward. "This is an outrage, Mr. Charon, but it is hardly the most important crime committed in the metropolis today. I suggest that you notify the widower before any enterprising newsmen get wind of this burglary. And you may wish to return the jewels to him as well; his son will certainly appreciate that several thousand pounds of the family fortune have been unearthed."

"But...you...Mr. Holmes! You know there is more. You *smelled* him!"

Holmes halted, turning slowly. I pivoted as well, and saw Charon's eyes grow wide.

"It is he, isn't it?" Charon insisted, his tone accusatory. "Spring Heeled Jack? He leaves sulphur in his wake, and brimstone is his breath."

"That is a tale for a winter's night, Mr. Charon," Holmes replied. "You would do well to watch your tongue."

"It's true, then," Charon spat, curling one fragile fist and shaking it at Holmes. "You have turned your back on your own kind, walked beyond the Shadows never to return?"

Holmes tipped his hat. "Good day, Mr. Charon. Watson...come."

I had no option but to follow.

Chapter Four

"Holmes," I said, late that same afternoon, when the Beaune I had consumed at luncheon rallied my courage, "if you truly value my assistance, you must confide in me. What did Charon mean by his strange words? Who is Spring Heeled Jack?"

Holmes turned from his deal-topped table and the chemical apparatus that he had been manipulating for several hours with grim, silent intensity. "Really, Watson, you disappoint me," he said, "I thought your knowledge of the penny dreadful was unsurpassed."

I refused to be baited. "Perhaps I missed that particular edition."

"Touché, Watson!" Holmes laughed, clapping his hands together. "You are certainly feeling more like yourself again."

I pulled the armchair up, making it clear to him that I would not be dislodged until he provided information. With a sigh of resignation, Holmes folded his arms and began to speak.

"Spring Heeled Jack is a figment of the popular imagination, Watson. He first appeared in 1837, and has had many notable moments on the stage since. He is rather enduring for a character who began as a molester of women."

I settled into the chair and nodded for Holmes to continue his story. The expression on his face told me that he was caught between the inclination to dismiss the tale as mere fantasy and the stronger urge to examine it as a case, dissect it for clues and suggestive elements. I knew from long experience that Holmes preferred the odd and unusual in life. The more bizarre and grotesque the scenario, the more intrigued Holmes would be.

"Almost a century ago, a servant girl was returning to her employer's home late at night. She was crossing Clapham Common when a dark figure attacked her from an alley. It seized her and kissed her, tore at her clothing with sharp claws. Her screams brought aid, but whatever it was---whether man or beast or devil was uncertain---it evaded capture by a most unusual method. The girl claimed that her assailant leapt into the air, made one or two great bounds, and disappeared."

"Preposterous!" I snorted.

Holmes' lips compressed tightly for a moment, as if he was tempted to agree with my assertion. Then he resumed the story, avoiding commentary. "But the very next evening, close by the victim's home, a coachman was attacked by this same monster. This time, the creature sprang directly into the path of the vehicle, causing the horses to rear and the carriage to overturn. The coachman barely escaped with his life and again witnesses on the scene reported that the villain escaped by

31

springing deftly over high walls and bounding across rooftops with supernatural speed and grace."

"So there were witnesses this time!" I interjected. The maid's story I could dismiss as a case of female hysterics, but the presence of masculine interlopers changed the tale completely.

"Yes, and all were considered calm, rational men," Holmes added, clearly reading my thoughts. "Since that day 'Spring Heeled Jack,' as the newsmen cleverly dubbed him, has frequently reappeared to make lewd assaults on women and cause fatal accidents to unwary nocturnal travellers."

I shook my head. "But surely there is some rational explanation."

Holmes nodded, picking up a beaker and toying with it as he spoke. "For a time, the Marquess of Waterford was suspected of the crimes."

This information surprised me. "A nobleman? Why would he be considered a suspect?"

"There is his Irish lineage against him," Holmes said, with a touch of amusement, "but he was already notorious for his brutal pranks and vandalism, as well as his drunkenness. However, unless he somehow contrived the ability to be in two places at one time, he could not be our villainous Jack. Over a hundred people saw the Marquess at a St. Valentine's Day Ball which occurred on the same evening as one of the most notorious attacks. There is also the strange fact that Spring Heeled Jack never seems to age, nor can any of the witnesses agree on his attire. Some say he wears a tight garment of white, much as an acrobat might don, while others say that he is clad like a gentleman, in high boots and a cape. Indeed, the only thing that all observers agree upon is Jack's malicious, ringing laughter, ability to leap over tall objects, and hellfire breath. It is said that he exhales fire and brimstone."

Charon's words echoed in my head. "Holmes, that was what your client said."

"And thus my response to that individual, Watson. He had best look for his thief among the stories and rumours. This is not a man of flesh and blood, but a legend born of some trickster's ingenious lark."

"But someone very real has stolen the body of Lady Ariel. Perhaps he donned the disguise of this character while doing so."

Holmes gave a distracted nod and turned back to his work. I rose and moved closer to stand behind him.

"But there were no witnesses who could point to Jack at Highgate cemetery. The only evidence is that Charon said that you smelled him."

"Ah. Do you mean to say you did not detect the whiff of sulphur in the air as well?"

"No, Holmes, I did not."

Holmes ignited a burner, began lining up his rack of test tubes. It was as clear a dismissal as he could give, especially with the words that followed.

"Then perhaps you are suffering from some congestion of the nasal cavities, because the odour was rather heavy. It would behoove you to consult a doctor."

I had wearied of Holmes' abrasive manner. I seized my coat and hat and departed.

Chapter Five

I resolved to eradicate my annoyance with Holmes by the means of another strenuous constitutional, a long walk that took me through many realms of the great metropolis. There was hardly a street or an alleyway or a building that did not remind me of some adventure I had shared with my friend. These sites, and their memories of happier times, plunged me into further melancholy as I tried to account for Holmes' behaviour. His coldness was something I had grown accustomed to. I am not the sort of man who needs reassurances of devotion, or even affection of any sort. But I did expect to be appreciated, for my doglike loyalty if nothing else. Holmes, for all his faults, appeared to genuinely value that trait in a companion. So what could account for his recent shift in temper? Why was he suddenly so curt and dismissive to me? Why did I sense that he would be glad to be rid of me, and would not object if I packed my valise and sought other lodgings?

It was in this dismal state of mind that I stumbled upon a man walking the streets, bearing a double-sided placard for a music hall amusement. Bold red letters spelled out SPRING HEELED JACK: THE TERROR OF LONDON. Beneath this text was a drawing of a man in high boots and a fusilier's shirt, a bat-like mask over his face. He held his arms aloft, with a winged cape flaring around them. Beneath him, a woman in a thin gown cowered, and behind him men with rifles took careful aim. Even lower were the words NOW PLAYING AT POWN'S MUSIC HALL. I was not acquainted with the establishment, and paused to ask the advertisement man for directions. I soon found myself in a dreary section of London not many blocks from Whitechapel. Pown's Music Hall looked to be cheap and crass. I almost turned away from this vulgar establishment, but then decided that by viewing the disreputable entertainment within I might uncover some vital clue as to the outrage at the cemetery, or at the least learn more about this Spring Heeled Jack character and his place in the gothic imagination.

The lights were just dimming for the matinee performance when I took my seat, having gained admission for a mere sixpence. I had barely time to glance around at the audience, which was a small one, comprised mainly of the toughs and louts that one might encounter on any street corner in this unsavoury neighbourhood. I was grateful for the sudden darkness that concealed my gentleman's attire, and out of caution I joined in with the hoots and shouting that accompanied the opening act, a 'ballet' of sorts, featuring young women in scanty clothing. What they lacked in dancing talent they made up for in lewd displays of breasts and thighs, much to the appreciation of the lads who sat on folding chairs near the footlights. After final kisses were blown, a moustachioed host strutted to the centre of the stage and announced that the next act would be the featured one, entitled 'The Revenge of Spring Heeled Jack.'

Ominous music drifted from the shallow pit just beneath the stage. The curtain rose again and a young woman, her face caked in freakishly white cosmetics, after the fashion of the beauties of the eighteenth century, appeared. Behind her was a brick wall labelled 'Low Gate Cemetery.' The young woman sang a ditty about her youth and innocence. Midway through the first verse, a figure suddenly appeared behind her, bounding just above the wall. Several members of the audience gasped, then began to laugh as it occurred, even to the dimmest among them, that the effect was achieved as the actor bounced on some variety of trampoline.

I leaned forward, impressed by the performer's agility. He was a young man, lithe and flexible, able to perform all manner of contortions while suspended in midair. He wore a white suit that clung to his slender frame, with slippers shaped into the form of rakish boots. A bright red coat, cut in a military style, completed his wardrobe. His face was covered with a devil's mask and once he appeared to exhale fire. As the girl's song ended, the character abruptly cleared the wall and landed just beside the girl, who feigned horror and revulsion.

"Come now, pretty maiden!" 'Jack' proclaimed, and I was astonished to realize that the figure I had taken for a lad was actually a young woman. "Won't you give Spring Heeled Jack a kiss?"

The girl shrieked. Jack seized her and pressed hungry lips to hers. The crude men around me cheered and clapped, and I found myself embarrassed that I had been lured into such a filthy entertainment. I started to rise from my seat when there was a cry of alarm. Three men, armed with pistols and rifles, rushed onto the stage. Jack released the victim, who crumpled to the floor in a swoon. With a wave of the cape and a shout of "You'll never catch me!" the imp sprang skyward as the guns roared.

I had expected such a dénouement, that the actress, tethered by wires, would be drawn up into the curtains. Instead, she flew outward, over the heads of the audience. For an instant she seemed to hover amid the rafters. Then she dropped down, landing lightly on a table, snatching a cap from a young ruffian before once again taking to the air. Five more times she descended and sprang, the audience now making every attempt to seize her, while she laughed at their clumsy antics. She dodged back to the stage, pirouetted atop the stone fence, and vanished in a puff of sulphurous smoke. The heavy curtain quickly descended.

A card announced that the next act would be 'Howler Harvey and His Clever Companion." A man in a chequered suit, carrying a large wooden doll dressed in a similar fashion, hurried onto the stage. I sought the aisle, grateful to escape from such a low establishment. As I reached the lobby a hand was suddenly on my arm.

"Doctor Watson, sir?"

It was the young woman from the entertainment, the one who had portrayed the defiled maiden. She was still in her costume, her face slathered with make-up. Her dress was even more immodest than it had appeared onstage. I forced my eyes away from her nearly naked breasts.

"Yes?"

"Miss Adler said it was you. She recognized you in the crowd. Won't you please come backstage and speak to her? She told me that you are old friends."

Readers of my works can only imagine what effect this invitation had on me. The remarkable Miss Irene Adler was the heroine of one of the first adventures I shared with Sherlock Holmes. Indeed, in his mind, she remained "the woman," holding that place not only for her beauty, but for her intelligence in beating Holmes at his own game. I could not have been more startled. To my knowledge, Miss Adler had married and lived a retired life. To find her on stage again, and in a gritty music hall, suggested a tragic turn of events. Even if my own curiosity had not been provoked, I felt that I owed it to Holmes to investigate.

"Of course," I answered. "Please, take me to her."

The girl led me through a curtained alcove and along a warren of corridors beneath the theatre. The narrow passageway was a riot of activity. Ballet girls in their skimpy costumes hurried past, and I stepped aside as a magician's brightly painted boxes were wheeled by. My guide finally opened a door and I was ushered into a small, overheated chamber. It was bare except for a heavy armchair, a dressing table, and a rack containing a large selection of costumes. The incomparable actress was sitting at the ornate wooden vanity table, still clad in her Spring Heeled Jack attire. She made a careless gesture at the chair and I sat in it, only vaguely aware that the door had closed and I was alone for the interview. I coughed nervously, clearing my throat.

"My dear Miss Adler, I…I ah…I had no idea that you had returned to your theatrical career and---"

Something contracted around my right wrist. I looked down and found that the wooden armrest of the chair had somehow wound itself over my limb. Before I could react, the opposite section of the furnishing, which was shaped in the head of a lion, also broke free and twisted around my left wrist. Something like a tail whipped around and formed a barrier across my chest. The chair tipped backwards, putting my feet above my head. I was so startled it took two attempts before I could produce coherent speech.

"My God, what---what is this!"

The actress turned and slowly removed her mask. The face beneath it was not that of the lovely opera diva, whose picture Holmes kept hidden away. Indeed, it was not the face of a woman at all, but that of a monster, with great grey scales in place of flesh, eyes that spat fire, and a green tongue that uncoiled from mucus covered lips until it fell upon the creature's chest.

I could not speak, or scream, and though I struggled in my mind, my body was as paralyzed as if I had been injected with some South American poison. I could only watch in horror as this thing from the bowels of hell rose from its perch, oozed to my side, and slowly bent over me, its claws prying open my mouth.

Chapter Six

"There's naught but the truth for it now, it seems."

It took all my strength just to lift my head. Holmes was standing a few steps away from me, idly examining the costumes dangling from the rack. I struggled to bring him into focus, fighting down nausea.

"The truth would, I believe, be the least that I deserve," I said to Holmes, with more than a touch of bitterness.

How does one describe a nightmare vicious enough to blot out all reality, one that plunged the dreamer into a Hades so horrific even the medieval artists of damnation could not properly illustrate its terrors? I had awakened from my stupor sure of only one thing---this nightmare was real.

I had been attacked by a creature mankind has yet to name, and this creature had taken something vital from me. I still shuddered at the remembrance of its slime-coated lips pressed to my own, of the great suction that consumed me as I was bound helpless to the chair. I had thought I would die; the pain was unbearable, like years of Ghazi torture slipped into a single instant. And then the monster had drawn away, spat into a small vial it held in its misshapen hand. I saw a blue light glow within the glass. The creature's hideous maw shaped into a smile and I heard a woman's sweet voice emerge from that foul being's depths.

"Our business is concluded, Doctor Watson. Let us hope that your friend is willing to make the deal we both so intimately desire."

And then she was gone in a puff of smoke, just as she had disappeared from the stage. Moments later, as I was still gasping and struggling in vain to free my limbs, the door had been kicked open and Holmes was on the threshold, a pistol in his hand.

Holmes stared at me for a moment and whispered my name. He extended his left hand and snapped his fingers. In that instant, the chair was transformed, I was free, and the room was an ordinary chamber, as if some invisible eraser had wiped the magic and horror away in a single swipe.

And now Holmes was standing silently, eyes locked to the tattered remnants of the costumes. Anger boiled up inside me, spewed into my words.

"Damn you, man! Some vile monster has attacked me and---"

"More than attacked, Watson. She has taken your last breath and with it your very soul."

I stared at him, dumbly repeating his words. "My soul?"

"To every mortal, only so many breaths are granted. On the very last one rides your immortal essence, waiting to spring back to the Creator's hands. If you died now, your soul would remain entrapped, a prisoner within that enchanted reliquary. You would never know hell or heaven, only great nothingness, the Void for all eternity."

Once again a kind of darkness threatened to consume me. I willed myself away from the comfort that it would offer. I forced myself to think and to question.

"Holmes...how can any of this be? I feel as if the world has suddenly been torn apart, that my understanding of it has been ripped into pieces."

"An apt metaphor, Watson. But do you remember what I said to you, only hours ago, when I spoke of the Shadows?"

It all returned in a rush, as if that single word had given permission for the memories to flood my consciousness, like water over a broken dam. "Yes. You said it was a world of its own, separated from ours by---"

"Mere atoms, Watson. Spaces between the spaces. A world much older than our own, wilder and more ferocious, a vast howling wilderness and a place where all the darker creatures of imagination have dominion." He took the performer's stool and sat down on it. "The world of the Shadows is hungry. Its beings will devour those of our world whenever they can."

"But if such a place exists," I said, still wincing against the rawness of my throat and the emotion of violation, "how can you know of it?"

44

His tight grimace was the saddest of smiles. "Because I was born there, Watson, and I can move between our world---the world of Sun---and the world of Shadows whenever I choose."

His simple statement hit me as if he had reached across and driven a great fist to my face. "What do you mean?"

He placed his elbows on his knees, linked his fingers together as he spoke. It was a gentle tone, almost soothing, yet every word caused prickles across my skin. "Watson---you have often wondered why I never speak of my people. It is because they do not exist in this world of Sun. To look upon the faces of my relations, I would have to journey into the Shadows, where those whose bloodlines I share reside."

For a long moment I could not find words, and when they at last came to me, they arrived with a viciousness I had not intended. They cut between us like knives.

"*What* are you, Holmes?"

"There is no true word for it, but the closest term would be a Merlin, a wizard. I inherited the powers of magic use from my mother's immortal house, even as I gained my height and my hair from my mortal father's."

"A wizard!"

This exclamation was greeted with a slight smile and a little bow of the head. "Indeed, Watson."

"Prove it," I ordered.

45

He nodded, as if he had expected my demand. Silently, he reached into his jacket and removed his silver cigarette case. He handed me a cigarette, replaced the case and told me to put the cigarette to my lips. I did so hesitantly, uncertain of what he wished to accomplish with this experiment.

Flame, orange and yellow, leapt from his index finger. I shied backward, but he caught my shoulder and held the burning digit to the end of the rolled tobacco. It began to smoulder. Holmes eased back, simply closed his hand. The fire was extinguished, and as he opened his hand again I saw that there was no damage, no change to his flesh. It was free of the expected rawness or raised blisters.

I shuddered and fixed my eyes on the slowly rising smoke from my cigarette. "Any Covent Garden conjurer could do the same."

"Perhaps. It is, of course, your choice as to whether you believe in me or not."

I dropped the cigarette. It hit the floor and vanished with a sparkle of red light. I stared at it for a long time, unable to develop any alternative explanation for such wonders. My friend was telling me the truth. "Before," I muttered, "the strange dream, followed by illness the next morning, were you responsible?"

Holmes stood and considered the rack of costumes. "Of course, Watson. After you took me unawares with Titania,

46

I thought it best to wipe the memory from your mind with a drugged sleep spell. But your brain, it appears, is much stronger than I imagined it to be."

"Thank you," I growled at him. "I am gratified by your high opinion of me."

Holmes took the barb silently. Then, with a violent motion, he knocked the rack of costumes to the floor.

"We had best be leaving, Watson. While it would do Titania no good to cause us injury, her sense of the perverse is astonishing in one so old."

"Titania? The fairy woman?"

"The High Queen herself. I should have known when I refused to assist her that she would do some mischief. I do owe you a thousand apologies, my dear Watson, but I never thought for a moment she would seek such a valuable hostage."

I was somehow pushing to my feet. I no longer ached, but I felt strange, as if somehow lighter, not as firmly attached to the earth by gravity as I should have been. "She was the creature that assaulted me?"

"It was she or one of her minions. No doubt we have been spied upon by her servants from the moment she abandoned us in Baker Street. Fairies have the skill to cloud men's minds, seduce them. She lured you in with a tale you were naturally curious about and made you vulnerable in order to steal your soul."

Before I could question, Holmes strode through the dressing room door, giving me no choice but to follow him. The passage back through the theatre was dull, unmemorable, and empty. "Holmes, if this awful thing is true," I said, as we made our way down dark and narrow corridors, "then how are we to retrieve what she has taken?"

"That is simplicity in itself, Watson. I must solve the riddle that Titania has put before me, come to her aid. Once that is done, she will give you back your soul."

"What makes you so certain?"

"Because fairies always keep their promises," Holmes replied, with a snarled laugh. "It is the only moral quality they possess."

He pushed a door open. I followed him onto a portico and then down a set of high steps that I did not remember ascending when I entered the music hall.

"Holmes," I pleaded, "please tell me that this is some delusion. Give me a stout cuff to the jaw or a good hard shake and make me wake from this awful dream."

He halted, considering me with infinite sadness. "I am sorry, old friend. I only wish it could be so."

"Holmes!" I protested, still not completely able or willing to believe that these terrible revelations were true.

"Look behind you," he instructed. Reluctantly, I turned and did as he bade.

There was no door, no steps, and no theatre. Indeed, there was only a brick wall and a set of boarded shutters high above. We were in the street, standing before a large, abandoned warehouse.

"But how—"

"You walk in Shadows now, Watson. Vanquish any hope of escaping them."

Chapter Seven

Holmes hailed a cab and we passed the journey back to Baker Street in silence. I watched the city's life flowing around me with a strange numbness, a detachment that was alien to my character. The workmen hurrying home, the couples walking arm in arm, the children skipping rope or tossing balls, they were as puppets to me. If they were only a tissue of reality, merely a reflection of one world instead of the sum of all worlds, then what was I? What did I matter? What difference would it make if my soul were never retrieved?

If we were only the food, helpless substance to the Shadows, then what was the point of mankind's very existence?

"Watson," Holmes said, just as we made the final turn toward our shared residence, "you must not give way to despair. That is the first and greatest weapon of the Shadows, the thing you must guard yourself against."

"But if my soul is gone then---"

I was poised to speak further, but Holmes glanced down the street and suddenly thudded his knuckles to the roof of the cab. Our driver pulled to an abrupt halt, his horse whinnying in protest. We disembarked a block away from our door, and I saw why Holmes had decided to lengthen our journey.

A handsome brougham was parked at our kerb. The driver was seated on his perch, wrapped in a long dark coat with his hat pulled low. The matched horses were coal black and showed refined breeding in every line. As we passed, Holmes nodded toward the gleaming coat of arms on the brougham's door.

"Good heavens," I whispered, "the Home Secretary."

"And a guest," Holmes noted, spotting some clue inside the elegant coach. "I fear I will have to disappoint Lord Snowfell."

"Holmes, you can not mean that. It might be a summons from the Queen herself."

"I have a far more important mission to fulfil," he said, putting a hand to the door of 221 B. "But, still, one can hardly afford to be rude to a man of such elevated status. Mycroft would never forgive me."

The mention of Holmes' brother brought another question bubbling to my lips, but at just that moment Mrs. Hudson stepped into the foyer, one hand on her hip and the other gesticulating unhappily at the upper floor.

"Mr. Holmes, the gentlemen would not take no for an answer! I told them they would have a long wait, but they insisted on seeing you."

Holmes nodded and started up the stairs. I followed at his heels, thinking once again how many personages of rank had climbed the seventeen steps to Holmes' modest sitting room. I could never forget the time we returned from a spring stroll and found none other than the Prime Minister smoking a cigar and glaring out our window.

The man who looked up from a dark study of our fireside carpet was perhaps the finest orator and most distinguished politician of the age. His deep blue eyes beneath iron grey brows held us each in turn, and I felt the sudden urge to offer a bow. Holmes barely inclined his head.

"Lord Snowfell, welcome. I apologize for my tardiness, but the good landlady warned you of such a possibility."

The great leader did not move, but scowled at us from his chair like the wizened god of an ancient wood. His skin was leathery and creased, the mark of his many years on campaigns in the most forsaken hellholes of the empire. He unfurled a lean hand and gestured sharply at Holmes.

"Whatever petty business you were upon, you must drop it, immediately."

Holmes folded his arms, addressing his words not to Lord Snowfell, but the second man, who stood in the shadows, his hat in his hands. He was stout and broad-shouldered, dressed so plainly in a dark suit that he was nearly invisible in the room's gloomy corner. "The Secretary speaks as if my agency is limited to locating missing hatpins or retrieving love letters," Holmes noted, "yet he would hardly have brought you, Mr. Cartwright, a warder of the Tower, to me if he truly believed my talents to be so limited."

The second man nodded and turned his hat round and round. "Why, that's true sir, I am one of the yeoman warders but how---"

"Any citizen may visit the Tower and recall the face of the man who gave him a tour," Lord Snowfell snapped. His eyes blazed at my friend. "It is not so impressive a trick."

Holmes barked a laugh. "Well done, sir. It speaks to your intelligence, if not your tact, to not be so readily amazed. And you will be less disappointed when I tell you that I have no intention of laying aside my current investigation for whatever conundrum or embarrassment the current regime finds itself in."

Lord Snowfell made an angry snort, like a bull preparing to charge, even as his body remained rigid in the chair. "You will not refuse me, Mr. Holmes. I come under orders from the Privy Council."

"In that case, do give those most esteemed gentlemen my most sincere regrets."

"You arrogant scoundrel! How dare you!"

"Mr. Holmes, the ravens, sir. You must help us--- they're gone!"

The sudden outburst from our otherwise timid guest took us all aback. The man stepped into the lamplight and I saw that his face was drawn in a mask of horror and agony. His pallor and nervous energy was a strange contrast to his solid frame. In his red and black uniform this guardian of the Tower would have been a formable force, but quivering and white-faced, he now presented a most piteous spectacle.

I turned to see what effect his trembling words had upon Holmes. I was nearly staggered by the reaction, for my friend had grown still and every trace of defiance was wiped away. He inclined his head, speaking softly.

"The ravens have abandoned the Tower?"

"Yes, Mr. Holmes. They have all disappeared."

Lord Snowfell flinched. "A foolish superstition, but this event has caused great alarm in the highest circles. I trust it sparks your interest, Mr. Holmes?"

"Watson, do pour Mr. Cartwright a brandy and soda. Now, sir, please be seated and let me have the story from the beginning."

The nervous warder looked to his superior, who gave him a curt nod. I handed him a drink as he settled onto the sofa.

"I am only a sergeant, sir, but my among my duties is a very special one. I am the ravenmaster to the Crown. My most important duty is to care for the seven great birds of the White

54

Tower. It is my job to protect them, keep their wings clipped, and feed them on a diet of raw meat and blood." He looked to me, fingers trembling around the glass. "Do you understand why the birds are so important?"

"There is some legend," I said, remembering an afternoon's diversion and the fantastic stories told by the uniformed guards. "A tale that should the ravens abandon the Tower the monarchy will fall."

"And all of England with it," Holmes added. "It would mean the end of an empire and an age."

Cartwright nodded. "There have always been ravens at the Tower. They were necessary in the times when executions were common, plucking apart the remains of traitor's heads. King Charles II disliked them and ordered them killed, only to be told of the raven prophecy by a soothsayer. He commanded their protection, and since that time the yeoman warders have guarded the birds like beloved children. The ravens are each named and cared for in illness, coddled as pets. They would eat from my hands."

He choked back a sob. Holmes pulled out a chair and sat across from him. I saw the first hint of impatience in his eyes.

"Yes, I understand, but let us cut to the heart of the matter. Where are the ravens lodged and when did they disappear?"

Cartwright flinched. "During the day the birds are loosed on Tower Green. At sundown, they are collected and placed in a large aviary constructed upon the site of the old menagerie. Last evening, I locked them up and gave them their food. This morning, just before dawn, I found them missing."

Holmes scowled and rubbed one hand over his jaw. "It is difficult to imagine a sanctuary more secure than the Tower of London."

"Indeed, sir. The night guards reported nothing unusual. There was no sound, no intrusion."

"Would the birds react to a stranger?" I asked.

Cartwright nodded vigorously. "Oh yes, the birds are much like watchdogs."

"And yet they made no sound," Holmes said, and for a moment a mischievous smile played on his lean features. "The curious incident of the ravens in the night-time, wouldn't you say, Watson?"

Lord Snowfell had reached the end of his patience. He rose and snatched his high silk hat from the mantel. "I have heard enough. I will make my report to the Council, that this entire business is nothing but a farce!"

"Mister Secretary," Holmes countered, "I think you would do better to allow Mr. Cartwright to finish his most remarkable narrative."

There was something in my friend's voice that seemed to affect the great politician. He reclaimed his chair sullenly. Holmes gave the warder a short nod and asked him to continue.

"I arrived an hour before dawn, Mr. Holmes. I clucked to the birds, as I always do, and there was no answer. I brought my lantern up and saw that the cage was empty, but the gate was still in place, and the lock upon it."

"Secure?"

"Yes. And I will swear it had not been tampered with."

"Who else has the key?"

"No one, sir. Just myself. I sleep with it beneath my pillow." He glanced around, as if expecting some mocking words from the Home Secretary. "These are very important birds, sir. I would guard them with my life."

"I have no doubt of that, good warder," Holmes said. "But think very carefully---were there any signs of distress in that cage? Any great shedding of feathers or splashes of blood?"

"There was one bit of blood upon the bars, sir, but not enough to show violence. It was just a smear, and I thought perhaps it was my own. I am always getting pecked and nipped by my birds, though they mean no harm in it, I swear."

Holmes considered this information before turning to the Home Secretary. "These are deep waters, Lord Snowfell."

"Bah! Some miscreant has taken the ravens, but they can easily be substituted and the public need not know. Even now, birds are being brought in from Whitborne House, to replace those that have disappeared."

My ears perked at the mention of the estate, the home of the recently widowed knight. Holmes's dark gaze flicked to me, but he spoke to Lord Snowfell.

"Why Whitborne House?"

The statesman shrugged. "They raise ravens there. Some business about the family crest, I believe."

"You'll help, won't you, sir?" Cartwright asked. My heart went out to the poor man, who---I now gathered---was more concerned about the fate of his feathered friends than any possible dismissal or punishment for neglect of duty. Holmes rose and offered his hand to the warder.

"I am at Her Majesty's government's service. I presume that gives me carte blanche?"

Behind Holmes' back, Lord Snowfell scowled, clearly uncomfortable with Holmes' presumption. But he could hardly dismiss such an important assignment, whatever his personal misgivings. "It does. Under the usual clauses and conditions."

"Very well. Please give my regards to the gentlemen at Whitehall. And, Mr. Cartwright," Holmes said, "as soon as you return to the Tower, remove the section of the cage stained with blood, wrap it securely in paper, and send it to me by your most trusted messenger. Say nothing of this to anyone, not even the Master of the Yeomen. Is that understood?"

"Yes, sir. And the new birds?"

"Treat them well," Holmes advised, "but whatever you do, never turn your back on them. For the sake of your life, when you are around them in their aviary, do not blink."

Chapter Eight

I surprised myself by how well I slept that evening. Exhaustion claimed me almost before Mrs. Hudson cleared away the dishes. I expected only nightmares, but instead I simply closed my eyes and time passed in a welcome haze. When I finally awoke, I felt oddly refreshed and yet somehow still too light, empty, as if something that I had never before been aware of was now missing from my body.

The thought that Holmes was right, that what had been taken was my soul, caused me a few anxious moments over the morning's ablutions. The razor wavered in my hand as the blade seemed greedy for my throat. I scolded myself, asking if this was how a surgeon of Her Majesty's army should behave. I plucked up my courage with old lectures, the voices of drill sergeants thundering in my brain. At last I resolved that whatever fate had in store for me, I could do no better than to face it with a British soldier's steel.

Holmes had already finished his breakfast and was busy with his chemical apparatus. A parcel lay unwrapped upon the table next to him. He favoured me with a nod, returning to his work.

"Is that the bar from the ravens' cage?" I asked.

"It is. I regret that Mr. Cartwright was unable to send me a larger sample. This is so small there will be no room for error."

I poured coffee and plucked listlessly at a pastry. "What type of experiment do you propose? Will you test it with an acid or a base?"

"Neither," Holmes said. He paused, tilting his head as if toying with an unexpected idea. "Watson---would you care to watch?"

My own knowledge of chemistry was elementary, rudimental, the bare grasp required for a man of medicine, a practitioner rather than a theorist. I said as much to Holmes, who merely smiled at me.

"This is not chemistry as the universities define it. This is a reduction of the essence of Shadow, a science that mortals rarely witness and never understand when they do."

Intrigued, I moved to stand behind his chair. Holmes held up the single section of cage bar, a piece of wood no thicker than a pencil, or longer than my index finger. I could barely make out a smudge of dark fluid upon its surface.

"Tell me, Watson, what do you know of ravens?" Holmes asked.

I shrugged. "Very little. They are large birds, carrion eaters, a common enough sight above graveyards and battlefields." I suppressed a shudder, thinking of the dark forms I had glimpsed hovering over the carnage at the Battle of Maitland. "Edgar Allan Poe produced a most remarkable poem about one."

"Is that all?"

I wondered what he wished me to say. "I suppose they are creatures that play into many folktales and superstitions. I attended a birth in the country once, where the child's withered grandmother wished to offer the infant his first drink from the skull of a raven, claiming it would give the child the gift of prophecy. I prevented such unsanitary nonsense, of course."

Holmes lifted a single eyebrow. "Of course."

"But what else is there, Holmes?"

My friend dropped the small bit of wood into a copper bowl. "What is it you *feel* when you look upon a raven, Watson?"

I considered his question carefully. "I feel a certain dread, a coldness as if..." It came to me suddenly, just what he was driving at. "I feel as if I had just walked beneath a shadow."

Holmes beamed at me in the way a mathematics teacher would smile at a pupil who had just solved a difficult equation. "It is a sensation you share with all mankind. A raven has long been a portent of death, an evil omen. Yet at the same time, it is accounted the oldest and wisest of all the creatures of the earth, a bearer of the second sight and a servant to the gods."

"Which gods?"

"Odin, for example, had two ravens, one named Huginn, or 'Thought,' and the other Muninn, or 'Memory.' They circled the world and brought Odin reports of mankind's follies. Lludd, the Welsh deity of the arts, also possessed a pair of the magical birds. The evil sorceress Morgan le Fey was said to command them, as did the Cailleach, the Scottish goddess of winter." He pushed the bowl to one side, leaned back in the chair and made a steeple of his long fingers. "In the distant past these dark birds were not always seen as the enemies of mortals. Bran the Blessed, the great Celtic protector of Britain, was accompanied by ravens even after his decapitation. When his head was buried at Tower Hill, his ravens remained to protect his beloved 'sceptred isle' from invasion. That is the true origin of the tale that the yeoman warders tell. How quaint that the merry monarch Charles II receives the credit for a Celtic god's sacrifice."

As always, I was astonished by the wide, yet eccentric, nature of my friend's knowledge. I had heard of none of these characters or legends. "Holmes, what are you implying?" I asked. "Are the ravens of the Tower somehow magical?"

"Perhaps. There are many creatures that belong to both the worlds, to Sun and to the Shadows, Watson. One sits before you." Before I could question or even absorb the impact of what he meant, he grabbed my wrist and drew a needle from his pocket. "Do forgive me," he whispered, and with no further preamble he plunged the sharp point into the tip of my index finger. I gave a shout of surprise. Holmes twisted my hand so that my wound dripped fat scarlet tears of blood into the bowl, coating the bit of wood within.

"What the devil will that prove?" I demanded.

"Perhaps nothing, or perhaps…"

I gasped. The material in the bowl had begun to smoke, as if my haemoglobin had ignited it. Holmes plucked a test tube from a rack, held it above the curling green vapours. As suddenly as it had begun, the combustion ceased, and Holmes fitted a rubber stopper over the glass. The smoke continued to spin and writhe, confined inside an instrument of science, even as the tube was returned to its metal rack.

"What does it mean?" I asked, barely aware that Holmes had removed his own handkerchief and had pressed it to my hand.

"It means that our friend the ravenmaster was not the one whose blood was left upon the cage. This blood belongs to a creature of the Shadows; what we witnessed is the expected reaction of Shadows blood to human blood." He rose and removed a pipe from the mantel, lighting it with a distracted motion. "Let us consider it logically, Watson. The Tower of London is well fortified, impervious to burglars and bird-snatchers. The birds made no cry and raised no alarm. As we have learned in our past adventures, lack of action has great significance. The ravens knew the one who came for them."

"So it must be the warder who committed the crime. He is lying about his involvement in it."

Holmes shook his head briskly. "He has no motive to commit such a deed. Consider the evidence I have just provided. A mere human fortification is no obstacle to a resident of the Shadows, yet he or she has been imprudent enough to leave one drop of blood behind. Now what suggests itself to you, especially in light of this information?"

I listed the evidence on my fingers. "The thief is someone the birds recognized. The figure is not human, as you have just proved, but a creature of the Shadows. Therefore the thief is a…" I hesitated, uncomfortable with the word I was about to use, "A god?"

"Or fairy or monster. Unfortunately our small experiment does not narrow the suspects as much as one would wish." Holmes moved to his index, pulling down a volume that was tattered and overflowing with clippings. "However, knowing the Shadows as I do, one name suggests itself. You will not be startled to learn, my dear Watson, that even as in the human world certain miscreants return consistently to their old ways and familiar crimes, beings of the Shadows also are known by their *modus operandi*."

He opened the volume, muttering to himself, before finally motioning me to his side.

"Did I not tell you that my collection under the letter M was a fine one? Look here."

I gazed down at the entry, which was illustrated with a drawing of a dark-haired woman in a gore-splattered gown, holding a great spear in her skeletal hand. Perched on her shoulder was a raven.

"*The Morrigan,*" I read aloud, "*the Celtic goddess of war, fate and death. During battles she flies above the field in the form of a raven, and chooses among the souls of the slain for dead men to rise again as her spectral warriors. Worshippers honour her with a red cloth, the feather of a crow or raven, and bowls of brine and blood.*"

Just as I completed my recitation, the door to the room banged open, so loudly and with such force that I nearly jumped in reaction. Holmes merely removed his pipe from his lips and gestured for our unannounced guest to enter and be seated.

"Good morning, Charon. You do look more frightful than usual---tell me, which body has disappeared from Highgate this time?"

His eyes bulged. His lips quivered and he dropped like a stone onto the sofa.

"<u>All</u> of them, Mr. Holmes."

66

Chapter Nine

It was a fantastic sight that greeted us as Charon unlocked the huge iron portals of Highgate Cemetery. Though brush and shrubbery hid the devastation from the view of pedestrians along Swains Lane, one had only to take a few steps beyond the ornamental trees and flowers to see the massive, appalling damage within the burial grounds. I thought at once of the diggings at Ballarat and the mole holes burrowed in the lawn of Pondicherry Lodge. Earth was overturned, stones were broken, and monuments were tipped on their sides. Great statues rested in segments, armless and decapitated. I felt the cold stone eyes of outraged angels glaring at me, as if demanding to know who had so rudely cast them down.

"And there was no alarm?" Holmes asked, signalling for Charon and me to remain in place as he approached the nearest empty grave. He moved around it carefully, as if fearful to disturb even the least clump of soil.

"None, Mr. Holmes. There is a caretaker who resides in a small house on the property, and he woke at five to find the sacred ground profaned. His wits have been driven from him."

"This is impossible," I whispered, as Holmes directed us to follow him along the avenue. Every mausoleum door stood open, all the gates to the crypts were battered aside. Caskets were open and emptied, both below and above the ground. "No one could move this many bodies and not be heard. Even if each corpse could be removed, think of the wagons it would require to cart them away."

"Indeed, it is, as you say, impossible. And once we eliminate the impossible, whatever remains, however improbable, must be the truth."

Charon twisted his hands together. "The Shadows are at work."

"Yes," Holmes agreed, with an air of chastisement. "This is not a human crime."

Charon spoke gruffly, his eyes narrowing as he considered Holmes. "And now do you still refuse to investigate?"

My friend simply shook his head. He turned and motioned toward the gate with his stick. "You will keep the barriers closed. Permit no more burials until this matter is resolved."

"But, Mr. Holmes, I can not keep out the public more than a day or two at the most. And then, when the empty tombs are seen…"

"There will be panic, which is exactly the reaction that someone in the Shadows wishes to cause. It is essential that I bring the matter to a speedy conclusion. More than your reputation is at stake." Holmes pulled a small notebook from inside his coat. He scribbled a few words, tearing off the sheet and handing it to Charon. "Take this to Scotland Yard and insist that it be delivered to Inspector Lestrade. He will post a guard here, around the clock, to keep out the curious. Perhaps we can prevent a scandal for at least a few days."

Charon nodded and hurried back toward the gates. I huddled deeper into my greatcoat, for the morning was wet and foggy.

"Holmes, how could anyone remove so many bodies? And not even bodies, but bones and debris?"

"Watson, as usual you miss the essential question. It is not how the corpses were taken that should concern us, but where."

"We can hardly know where if we do not know how," I protested, with some testiness. "Are we tracking ghostly wagons, or horses, or trains that float upon the air?"

He chuckled. "Your spirit is to your credit, Watson."

"Holmes," I muttered, more than a little chagrined by his treatment.

"I promise, all things in time," he said, with a moderately apologetic smile. "But for now, let us concern ourselves with following the path of the remains. And for this, I must call upon my familiar."

I shook my head, confused by his terminology. "I do not understand."

"Every magic-wielder has a familiar, Watson. A creature bound to him, to do his bidding, to assist in his spell casting."

"Like a black cat for a witch?"

"A cat, a dog, a bird---even frogs have had their vogue. Mine is perhaps a more prosaic choice."

He reached inside his coat and removed his cigarette case. He spoke a word in an unknown language as he waved his hand over the silver box. The container suddenly shone like a beacon, brighter than any lantern, and I turned aside, eyes burning. There was a click as he opened it, and a tiny point of golden light shot from the container. I heard a sound like a great buzzing.

"Holmes, is that an insect?"

"It is the humble *apis mellifera,* or western honeybee. He is noted for his industry and strength and unfailing ability to find that for which he seeks." Holmes held out his palm, and the creature descended onto his flesh, wings drawn back against its striped body, still glowing with an unnatural light. "I will set him upon a trail---not for nectar, but for mortal dust. He will take us where ever the residents of Highgate have been so unceremoniously removed."

"But I still do not understand," I whispered, as I watched my friend give the slightly furred thorax of the creature a gentle stroke, "how could such a vast number of bodies be removed without anyone noticing? We are in the suburbs of London, not on the howling moors."

"You still fail to adequately apply my maxim," Holmes reminded, with a touch of asperity. "If it is impossible for such a task to be completed in this world---the realm of the Sun---without causing comment, then it can only mean that the job was undertaken in another world."

I began to understand. "The bodies went through the Shadows."

"Exactly, Watson. And through them we must pass as well, with our little friend as a guide." He moved to an open mausoleum, which resembled a stone temple robbed of its grim treasure. He held the honeybee inside, whispering more words in his strange tongue. The creature suddenly took flight, trailing brilliant gold flecks as it spun through the air. "No time to waste," Holmes urged. "I hope your old wound will stand it!"

In truth, I had forgotten the jezail bullet that had once pierced my thigh. There was something so fantastic, so utterly astounding about chasing after that pinpoint with the power of the sun bursting from its body that I felt I could have run a marathon and not tired. We bounded down the narrow lanes, barely avoiding the gaping wounds in the earth, climbing higher and higher on the hill until at last we reached the great pylons of the Egyptian Avenue. Holmes hesitated there, sensing something in the bee's progress.

"Here I must cross over, Watson. From this point, the Shadows must be breached. It would perhaps be safer, old friend, if you stayed behind."

"Don't be absurd, Holmes! You don't think for a moment I would turn back now, do you?"

His lips tightened. "No indeed. You are truly an old campaigner."

With a wink, Holmes knelt, scooping up a handful of cemetery dirt. He whispered soft words and then blew across the soil before flinging it into the air. It caught there, sparkling in flakes of silver and mica. I saw how the air behind it rippled like a great curtain, and all that was beyond that veil of earth seemed to melt, blending into an impenetrable darkness.

Holmes stepped forward and, with a deep breath of determination, I blindly trod in his footsteps.

Chapter Ten

We made slow progress through an inky world, a domain where I could feel but not see the things that passed by me, brushing my coat and swirling about my head. Each touch generated a wave of revulsion and a sensation of sickness. Whenever I thought I could discern a shape or a point of reference, it abruptly vanished, became a seamless part of the eternal night. I was guided only by the sound of our steps and the sensation of Holmes close to my side. It required all my courage not to reach out and seize his arm, to stay tethered to him as we moved through the complete blackness.

"Holmes," I asked, shuddering as yet some other gauzy but unseen thing caressed my cheek, "how vast is this territory?"

"Further than the human mind can comprehend, Watson. It overlays the earth, and sinks below the surface to incorporate hell. It expands into space to encircle the stars. It is everywhere reality is, and yet it is not."

Holmes spoke as calmly and dryly as if we were both ensconced in our rooms, chatting over brandies and cigars, discussing an election or even a rugby match, not such mystical and magical conundrums. The bee-light continued to flicker just ahead of us, our only illumination.

"This is but a small portion of the Shadows, Watson, a kind of tunnel through them from one destination to another. No doubt it was conjured by our culprits, to assist in their robbery."

"So we will emerge where they exited?"

"Yes."

"But if distance is irrelevant…"

"Precisely, Watson. We may arrive on a street in London, or Paris, or in the reception hall of the Emperor of Japan."

"If so, then I hope the tunnel is available for our retreat."

I heard him chuckle. "If not, I am capable of creating one. You are fortunate in that regard."

"It is not a common talent?" I asked, finding myself even more intrigued by these tiny scraps of information about my friend's powers.

"No. Only the most accomplished wizards and witches can even part the veil between the worlds," Holmes told me. "This is fortunate, for if the many denizens of the Shadows all possessed such abilities, the world of Sun would be overrun with monsters."

That revelation was so astonishing that I nearly lost my step, which would have been a very foolish action in that dark and dismal region. "So the monsters that the human world has known, they are escapees from the Shadows?"

"Exactly, Watson. The fiends which have haunted humanity across the ages---the vampires, banshees, werewolves and dragons---are creatures briefly loosed from the dark realm. And perhaps these encounters with the Shadows served a higher purpose. Otherwise, mankind would not have developed such rich, vivid mythologies."

More questions tumbled around in my brain. "Holmes, if you are a wizard born in the Shadows how did you come to live in Baker Street and hang your shingle as a consulting detective?"

For another moment all I could hear was our footsteps, which echoed hollowly in that undefined space. "Are you certain you wish to know the answer to that inquiry, Watson?"

"It seems a bit late to ask for ignorance now!" I snorted.

I had to imagine the smile I could not see. "My mother is a Fairy named Dana, the Sweet Lady of the Earth. She is one of the Protectors of the Shadows. But she loved a mortal man, and took the guise of a human woman in order to be his wife and bear him children. My elder brother, Mycroft, was born in realm of Sun, but shortly after my conception, Dana's consort was murdered. Upon my father's death, my mother fled back into the Shadows, where I was born. Both Mycroft and I were raised among the fairies, and trained in their arts, though I possess the greater gift for magic, as I was actually delivered within the Shadows realm."

I struggled to compose words to express my wonder at this tale. "So you are half mortal?"

"Indeed. While I am here, I am just as mortal as you are. And I will die as all mortals do, if I remain within the world of Sun."

I was curious about a thousand things, and was eager to hear more of his story. Yet one question superseded all the rest. I spat it out without thinking.

"So why have you chosen the world of Sun? Holmes, with your intelligence, your skills, you could rule the Shadows if you wished---and live forever!"

He stopped walking. I felt a sudden, cold pressure upon my arm. Just beyond us, the golden bee-light winked in rapid succession, but with a pattern, as if tapping out Morse code.

"We have arrived."

There was a rush of air as Holmes moved forward. I could sense but not see that he was waving his arms, once again creating some type of curtain to be lifted for us. By degrees, the light returned, and I could make out an image of a long, narrow road, lined on either side by sturdy elms. Holmes drew me through the shimmering division, and suddenly we were standing on the grounds of a great manor house. I whirled and looked behind me, saw nothing except an empty country lane. The day was bright but cool, and judging from the position of the sun, time had passed. We had emerged in mid-afternoon.

"But we have only been walking for twenty minutes," I protested, with a quick glance to my watch. Holmes pulled out a cigarette and lit it.

"Time, like space, has no meaning in the Shadows."

I accepted this as best my feeble brain could comprehend it. "So where are we?" I asked.

"That, my good Watson, remains to be discovered." Holmes held open the cigarette case, coaxing his magical guide back within it and returning the case to his pocket. "Judging by the flora and the temperature and the building I perceive in the distance, I would say we have arrived at some variety of English plantation. In fact, if the odd Tudor façade and Norman wings are to be recalled, this is Whitborne House."

"But Lady Ariel was the first victim. Do you suggest that her widower stole her body from the grave?"

"Watson, what leaps of logic you are making today!" Holmes chuckled. "I suggest nothing without further data, though I confess your speculation is intriguing. And it gives us the perfect excuse to pay a call upon Sir James, does it not?"

I nodded, wishing all the while that I could learn to master my urge to speak my own deductions. It was a failing I had acquired while attending Holmes, and one I blamed on him. Brilliance stimulates envy and competition in others; I wanted to show him what I had learned. But I would always, inevitably, miss the mark in some humiliating fashion.

The narrow driveway stretched a quarter of a mile. The manor was an imposing one, though as we drew closer we saw the signs of age and neglect in a crumbling western wall and broken glass in high windows. There was construction, or perhaps repairs, being undertaken on the eastern side, where the drive was littered with wagons and exhausted looking horses. We heard the sound of hammers and workmen's oaths. The lawn surrounding the home was overgrown with weeds. An ancient fountain choked with algae and wild lotus blossoms marred what might have been a picturesque view.

I wondered if this was a symptom of recent bereavement. Certainly in the weeks after my beloved Mary was so brutally taken from me, I cared not whether my small house was clean or the windows washed. I had only desired to shut myself in a dark room and wail for hours on end.

"You are correct, Watson---the neglect of the manor could be nothing more than an expression of a widower's grief. Though, if that is the case," Holmes said, continuing on as if he had not just read my mind, "one wonders about the nature of the repairs. Perhaps...."

Leaving his sentence dangling, Holmes turned on his heel and approached one of the sweaty workmen. The man looked up, wiped his face with a handkerchief, and generally gave the impression of an underling startled by the sudden approach of a superior.

"Here now," Holmes snapped. "I thought you would be further along. What is the delay? The firm's good name is at stake!"

"Yes, guv'nor, of course," the man said, cringing as he stuffed his handkerchief back into his canvas trousers. "And we will finish before tomorrow's done, that is certain. We'll finish or my name isn't Alonzo."

Holmes scowled, folding his arms. It was a testament to the force of his personality that the foreman never asked to see his credentials. "Why has progress slowed?"

"To be honest, sir---it was the smell!"

"The smell?"

"A great stench, sir. When we came on the site this morning, cor, it was like all the cemeteries in London was opened at once. Half my men was puking sick with it, sir. But then the fog lifted and took whatever it was away. We'll make up the time, sir, don't you worry."

Holmes gave a sharp nod. "See that you do. *Allons-y*, Alonzo!"

The man saluted and marched away, haranguing his troops as Holmes had scolded him. Holmes walked back to me with an arch grin.

"No magic was necessary, as you witnessed."

At that moment, I began to understand why he had returned to the world of the Sun. Magic and enchantments were less satisfying to him than the superb command of his own intelligence. There was a greater thrill in being a reasoning machine than in wielding supernatural forces.

"Will you be burgling the house as well?" I asked, with some amusement.

Holmes shook his head. "I think knocking will serve for the moment."

We approached the massive oaken door, with its brass knocker shaped as the head of a satyr. Before Holmes could lift the heavy instrument, the portal swung open and a young, dark haired man in his shirt sleeves stood just a pace before us, pointing a pistol squarely at our chests.

Chapter Eleven

"Good afternoon, Mr. Robert Whitborne," Holmes said, as casually as if he had encountered the fellow at a gentleman's club, instead of across the barrel of a gun. "Please lower your weapon. I assure you that we are not reporters."

"How do I know that? Do you have some proof of your identity?" the gun-wielder demanded. His eyes were red-rimmed, and I noted with trepidation bordering on alarm how violently the hand that held the pistol trembled.

"If you will permit me to withdraw my card without being mortally wounded?" Holmes asked. Whitborne nodded. Holmes reached into his jacket and presented the man with a cream-colored card. "As you see upon the stationary, my name is Sherringford Sigerson, and this is my associate, Doctor John Smith. We have come at the request of the Highgate Cemetery Company, to speak with you about the matter of the outrage perpetuated upon your stepmother's corpse."

The double aliases took me by surprise, but I worked to keep my features neutral. Whitborne thrust the card back, not to Holmes but to me, and I could not resist a glance at it. Much to my astonishment, the words *Sherlock Holmes, Baker Street* were clearly visible.

But Whitborne had lowered his pistol and was extending a hand to Holmes. A shamed look fell upon the young man's haggard features.

"Forgive me, Mr. Sigerson, Doctor. We have had nothing but nuisances for the past day, since those hellhounds of the press got word there had been a grave robbing. Please, come with me."

He gestured for us to follow him into the house. We moved rapidly, and I had only fleeting glimpses of a stately abode in the Tudor style, complete with a suit of armour in the hall and crossed swords and axes above the mantels. There was a certain dreariness to the place, an aura of decay, and the air was stale and dusty. No servants presented themselves. Whitborne escorted us into a small study, waved us into musty antique chairs, then poured us both glasses of what proved to be a most excellent port. Only when he had finished did a tall, dark-skinned man clad in a butler's livery appear in the doorway, offering a bow. I noted that the man had wads of cotton stuffed into his nostrils, as if suffering from some severe bleeding of the nasal cavities.

"May I be of service, Master Robert?"

Our host sent him away with a grumble. The moment he had exited, Whitborne tossed back half his glass. "That is Samedi, my stepmother's butler. He served her in America, but he's an odd fellow and I will be glad to be rid of him shortly. Now, what brings you gentlemen here? Has the company any news?"

"I fear not," Holmes said, with all the hushed reserve of an undertaker discussing delicate and morbid affairs. "We thought that perhaps the family had been approached, some ransom demanded."

"We have heard nothing," Whitborne said. "I have kept it from my father, of course. I believe the shock would kill him, in his fragile condition."

"Your father is ill?" I asked, having read nothing in the papers of a medical crisis in the home.

"He has grieved himself into a state of catatonia," young Whitborne stated. He seemed sincere in his words and in his expression of concern. His pale, exhausted face gave testimony to long hours spent caring for an invalid. "My father has barely slept or eaten since her death. I always knew she would bring him nothing but misfortune."

"You had no fondness for your stepmother?" Holmes inquired. Whitborne swallowed the last of his liquor and poured a second round.

"I'll tell no falsehood, sir. The woman was nothing but a strumpet, an American Jezebel. My father met her on a holiday in New Orleans, and she attached herself to him like a leech. She played my father for a fool and mocked my good mother's memory. She never loved him, only his money, and yet when I tried to make him see reason, he threw me out. I felt I had no choice but to leave the country. I returned as soon as I learned of her death, only to find my father in a terrible state of grief. I have cared for him day and night ever since."

"How did Lady Whitborne die?" I asked, a question that earned me a sharp glare from Holmes. I realized why even as I waited for a response; as a representative of the cemetery company, I should have known the cause of her death. Fortunately, the high flush to Whitborne's face suggested that he had already been at the port before our arrival and was not in a clear enough state of mind to reason out my folly.

"She fell down a set of stairs in the west wing of the house. To be candid, I suspect some quarrel took place between she and her servant." Whitborne gave an ugly laugh. "A lover's quarrel, if you will. I have always suspected them; they were far too close and more than once I noted a secret embrace in a shadowed hallway. I told my father what I had seen, but he was completely in her power. She held him spellbound."

Holmes lifted one expressive eyebrow, but his words were dry and clinical. "There was no investigation?"

Whitborne shrugged. "An inspector asked a few questions of the servants, but was satisfied that her death was accidental. I do not care to drag my father into a scandal by demanding a more thorough examination. It's bad enough about the money."

"The money?" I blurted, again wishing I had kept silent when I saw a deep flush bloom on the young man's face.

"Yes. Our fortune is nearly gone, but I'll be damned if I know where it went! My stepmother made large withdrawals before her death, and spent it all, somehow." He dropped his head and scuffed his hands through his hair. "Even now, there's work being done on the house that I did not order, but has already been paid for! They're tearing out rooms, building a kind of barn in our house. I wanted it stopped, but my father—in the only words he's spoken since I returned---forbade it."

"Was it also your father who ordered the ravens of Whitborne House sent to the Tower?" Holmes asked. The young man's reaction was a strange one. A kind of blankness came over his face, and he answered mechanically, speaking with a strange, jerky tone.

"I---no---there are no ravens here. I---do not know what you are---talking about."

Holmes nodded, as if he had expected exactly that bizarre reply. "Perhaps we might speak with your father?" Holmes suggested.

Whitborne blinked, like a man snapping out of a trance. He looked at Holmes, his eyes unfriendly. "What good could come of that?"

"My colleague has had remarkable success with alleviating disturbances of the mind," Holmes assured him. "Maybe you have heard of cases of premature burial where the victim had merely sunken into a strange coma? My friend has saved the lives of several persons who, had he not intervened, might have been surrendered to the grave while still breathing."

Whitborne shuddered. "To think that such horrors still occur in the modern world. Yes, Doctor...what did you say your name was?"

Damned if I had not forgotten it. Holmes intervened.

"Smith."

"Ah, of course...you may see him, Doctor Smith, but I beg you not to tax him or speak of this embarrassment. It is as much as I can do to force food and water down his throat."

"I will do what I can," I assured him, all the while regretting the absence of my medical bag. Young Whitborne led us upstairs and opened a locked door.

"Perhaps you think me cruel to confine him like a prisoner, but only a few days after my return I found him upon the very stairway where my stepmother fell, as if determined to do away with himself. Since then he has slipped into this trance, but I felt it best to take precautions."

I babbled for a bit, applauding his good sense in locking his father away. It had naturally dawned on me that Holmes had little curiosity about the invalid, but a great interest in the room in which he lived. Understanding that my part in the charade was to give Holmes as much time as possible in which to make observations, I made a close study of my patient.

Sir James Whitborne looked more like an elder of ninety than a formerly vigorous man in his sixties. He sat slumped in a chair, clad in pyjamas, with a checked wool blanket around his skeletal shoulders. His chest was concave, his hair had almost completely fallen out, and his dark blue eyes were fixed and vacant. Some crusts of his last meal clung piteously to his dried and cracked lips. His skin was liver-splotched, his nails long and pointed. I made a production of taking his pulse and listening to his heart, for by good fortune I had stored my stethoscope in my coat pocket. I heard no abnormal congestion; indeed, were it not for the evidence before me I would have assumed him to be a hale and healthy specimen, judging by the steady rhythm of his heart alone. All the time, I was aware of Robert Whitborne's intense scrutiny, how he watched my every action as if fearful that I would do his father some harm. I was also aware, at a distance, of Holmes edging about the spartan bedchamber. A sharp cough from him told me that I need not prolong my pantomime.

"Well?" the son asked. "What can you tell me?"

"I fear this is a hopeless case," I said. "You have done well to keep him comfortable. His mind will either heal itself, or he will shortly be out of all pain."

The heir nodded, looking as if he might burst into sobs at any moment. Holmes put a hand to his shoulder.

"We are sorry for your loss, and will not rest until we had found the answers we seek. Nor will we disturb you again until we have pertinent information. Good day, Mr. Whitborne. I believe we can see ourselves out."

Robert Whitborne dismissed us with a wave, and as I closed the door it was to the piteous scene of a man in the prime of life kneeling and weeping in his father's lap.

"Quickly," Holmes whispered in my ear, "we have not a moment to lose."

We hurried down the stairs. Holmes, with his refined sense of direction, set a course for the eastern confines of the house. But we had only just slipped into the passage when the Negro servant blocked our path. He was a head taller than Holmes, and though rather thin, he did not look like a man to be trifled with.

"May I assist you, gentlemen?" he rumbled.

"Yes, we seem to have taken a wrong turn," Holmes said, as carelessly as if his words were true. "I believe the manor may be exited this way?"

Samedi's features drew into a scowl. "It is closer in the other direction. I must insist that you follow me."

His tone indicated that he could be neither bullied nor bribed. Holmes seemed to take the setback in stride.

"I say, we encountered some workers outside. Can you tell me what firm they were with?" Holmes asked cheerfully. "I have need of repairs on my own holdings, and they seemed to be a handy lot."

"That is Master Robert's business, sir, and I do not speak of his doings. I bid you good day."

The door slammed behind us. It was almost twilight. The workmen had already departed, depriving us of an opportunity to cajole a ride with them to the nearest train station. However, one wagon remained behind, and Holmes walked over to study it. A flap of canvas covered the side. Holmes tore it back, so that we could read the business advertisement painted on the boards.

"One wonders who requires the services of a goldsmith at such an hour." Holmes muttered. "The entranced father, the angry son, or the mysterious foreign servant?"

"Or," I added, in hopes of lightening the grim mood, "perhaps it is the lady of the house, requiring some new finery to celebrate her return home." I immediately felt ashamed of myself for saying such a flippant thing, especially when my

89

friend's face drew into a thoughtful scowl. "Forgive me, Holmes," I apologized.

"Why should I?" Holmes whispered, "Especially when you may well be right?"

Chapter Twelve

After a long walk, during which Holmes brooded and smoked every cigarette within his case, we found ourselves at a small train station on the line between Oxford and Reading. Though it made for a footsore journey, I was secretly grateful that Holmes had not offered to open another tunnel through the Shadows. Just thinking of that lightless, airless place caused me to shudder. I hoped to never cross its threshold again.

As I waited, Holmes dispatched a series of telegrams. True to his custom, he did not reveal their contents to me. The man could be maddeningly secretive at times, a trait that his revelation about his hidden life had not altered in the least. We had a quarter of an hour to kill, and passed it on the empty platform searching for the distant light in the deepening darkness.

"Holmes," I said when the silence between us at last became unbearable, "you have never told me what she wanted."

"What do you mean?"

"Titania. What did she wish you to investigate? Not that it should deter you from the path you are already on, of course."

Holmes fished around in his coat and came up with an old and particularly noxious pipe. "Such will not be necessary, for I am convinced that our cases have merged. Titania has engaged me to find and return her crown."

"Her crown? A diadem?"

"It is the most priceless artefact in the world of the Fae, as they call themselves, Watson. It is a crown made from the first tears shed by every fairy infant upon birth. The tears transform into diamonds which are more priceless than all the jewels in the Tower of London's vaults. The loss of this artefact would be devastating to Titania, and perhaps lead to a royal crisis. By the law of the fairies, Titania must wear the crown on Midsummer's Eve if she wishes to retain her authority."

"So one of her rivals must have taken it."

"That struck me as the most likely possibility. Perhaps I am a coward, Watson, but I have no wish to meddle in the politics of the fairies. They may look beautiful and enchanting, but more callous, backbiting creatures have never been born."

"Yet you are..." It seemed rude to finish the sentence. Holmes snorted.

"Half-Fae. Yes, Watson, and am I not proof of my very own words?" he sneered. "Vicious, rude, and unfeeling."

"I would hardly go that far," I gently chided. "You are a bit rude perhaps, but otherwise you have never been anything but the wisest and most honourable man I have ever known."

Holmes lapsed into silence, with his head down, as if sunk into deep thought. Minutes crept by, lame and halting, like a pack of wounded soldiers. At last, in the distance, the train whistle blew. Holmes looked up slowly. He considered me for a long moment, and then spoke softly.

"Of all the many things that I have been granted, that I did not deserve, the greatest was you, Watson. But enough of this blather, we are due back in the metropolis. I will wager you five pounds that when we return to Baker Street, we will drown in correspondence."

"Indeed," I asked, as I rose and stretched my cramped limbs, "from whom?"

"Lestrade, for one, expressing his sulkiness over being ordered to post a guard at Highgate and enforce the company's moratorium on burials. He will want to know what the devil is amiss, but I will avoid addressing the issue of Old Scratch for as long as possible. As for the others, I expect....but here we are."

We boarded the train and returned to Baker Street without further incident or even conversation. When I at last opened the door of the sitting room, I was grateful that I had not taken Holmes up on his wager, lest my own purse be considerably lightened.

A number of envelopes were stacked upon the breakfast table. Holmes threw off his coat and ripped into them, asking me to do the same and read aloud the contents. I was astounded by the seal of office attached to one of the messages.

"Don't gape, man, read!"

I coughed and began my recitation with a letter from the Lord Mayor of London. *"Mr. Holmes, I must speak with you on a matter of some embarrassment. The London Stone has gone missing, and I believe that no other agency has the skill and discretion required to retrieve it."* I scowled. "What is the London Stone? I have never heard of such a thing."

"A large and otherwise innocuous rock," Holmes answered, slicing open a second missive, "said to have been part of an altar built by Brutus of Troy, the legendary founder of our fair city."

"London was established by a Trojan?" I asked, absolutely confounded by his obscure reference.

"Why Watson, do you mean to tell me that you are not up on your Geoffrey of Monmouth? That you have never read the *Historia Regum Britanniae?*" Holmes mockingly demanded. I was grateful that my ignorance gave him pleasure. I would gladly make the sacrifice of my dignity to lift the grim mood he had been in since abandoning Whitborne House.

"I fear my schoolboy days are long behind me, Holmes. Pray, enlighten me."

Holmes obediently began a narration. "Brutus was a descendant of the legendary Aeneas, a great-grandson if memory serves, and before he was born a magician prophesied that this child would rise to greatness, but only after he murdered both his mother and father."

"A cruel fortune," I commented.

"Especially for his mother, who died in childbed, and his father, who the child accidentally dispatched with a toy bow and arrow," Holmes agreed, not bothering to keep a trace of smug amusement from his tone. "Sensible relatives banished the boy from Italy, but after numerous adventures, mixed with a bit of Diana's divine guidance, he and his followers found their way to the mysterious island of Albion, in the western sea. Brutus and his warriors defeated Albion's native giants and established their own race upon the land, which was renamed in his honour."

"Britain," I said. "How absurdly simple. What a shame the legend is rarely recounted."

"But it was not lost. Even now, there are those among us who still worship the deities of Olympus, and who keep the flame of veneration alive for Greek and Roman heroes. If you look carefully in many of England's respectable households, behind nooks and crannies now covered over with excessive potted palms and velvet drapes, you will find shrines to Diana or Apollo."

"But what does this have to do with a stone?" I asked, deciding not to try to imagine couples attending services at Westminster Abbey before hurrying home to pour libations before household gods. The thought was simply too disturbing to me.

"'So long as the stone of Brutus is safe, so long shall London flourish' or so the prophecy goes," Holmes explained. "This stone has for decades been on discreet display in a box set into the wall of St. Swithin's Church, where it was considered nothing more than a quaint relic of a superstitious age." A smirk twitched Holmes' lips. "Of course, some people are aware of its importance. Every Lord Mayor of London is secretly charged with protecting it."

"And now it has been stolen."

"So it appears. Is there more to the message?"

I looked back to the paper I had nearly crumpled in my hand. "Yes, it continues—*The church had been secured for the night. When the chaplain went back inside, to retrieve a Bible, he found the glass display box broken and the stone removed. Please come as soon as possible.*"

Holmes made a steeple of his fingers. "That is suggestive."

"What is?"

"The broken box. That is the human way to remove an object one desires, to shatter the container and run off with it!

This implies that a human, not a creature of the Shadows---hello? What's this?"

The door to our rooms had been thrown open. A tall man in formal Scottish regalia stood there, his arms folded across his broad chest and his face drawn into a fierce scowl. Mrs. Hudson stepped out of the space behind him, grasping the front of her dressing gown with one hand and a candle with the other. Her nightcap was askew and her hair fell in a long, messy braid. She had clearly been dragged from bed and was not the least bit happy about the interruption to her well-earned rest.

"See here, Mr. Holmes, I TOLD him it was too late, that he'd have to come back in the morning! But just barged in he did, right past me, though I can't say how!"

Holmes rose, studying the strange figure in the doorway. I marvelled that anyone would be about in such a costume, especially on a chilly spring night. "It is quite all right, Mrs. Hudson," Holmes said, "I will receive him. And I do apologize for his intrusion."

Our landlady harrumphed and departed, taking her candlelight with her. Yet there still seemed an after effect of it, a strange glow that surrounded the silent, kilt-clad gentleman on our threshold.

"Please come in," Holmes said, with a fluid gesture. "How may I be of service to Mr. John Brown, servant of our Queen?"

Chapter Thirteen

For a moment I thought Holmes was making some kind of odd jest. Then I looked at the man more closely, and his face was at once familiar to me.

John Brown, the Scotsman, a *ghillie*, as outdoor servants are known in that country. I recalled the many stories and rumours that had swirled about him. He worked at Balmoral Castle, where the Queen became much attached to him after the death of her consort, Prince Albert. Brown was said to have been rude and gruff to our gracious majesty, treating her with crude but protective respect during her initial widowhood. Remarkably, she grew fond of Brown's brusque manner and he soon became not only her favoured servant, but a close friend and confidant. The Queen's children and advisors made it clear that they were disgusted by the Queen's choice of companion, and scandalmongers hinted that the couple had married, or lived together in a most indecent way. Our gracious majesty, of course, ignored such scurrilous talk and held Brown close for years. I had only a few days before read that the Queen retained his portrait upon her writing desk.

It was as close as she could keep him, for John Brown, servant and possible paramour to the Queen, had died in 1883.

Before I could pose any questions, the man marched into our room with the authority of a general. He scowled at the sideboard.

"Will ye not offer a drink to a man abroad on a foul night?"

Surely he was not a ghost or spirit. He seemed solid enough, even if he did emit an unnatural form of light. I watched as Holmes, with some amusement, poured a sifter of brandy for him. Brown tossed it back and licked his lips.

Much to my astonishment, there was no movement of his throat. He did not swallow. He handed the glass back to Holmes, and then reached into his stiff jacket, removing a folded paper. "Ye are summoned," he said, striding over to warm his large frame at the fire. When he stepped away, I saw two moist spots on the carpet where he had stood. The brandy had presumably gone right through him, exiting via the soles of his feet and saturating the rug.

My friend unfolded the note and quickly read the contents. He looked to the figure by the fire. "Not without Watson," Holmes said.

John Brown snorted. "Nay. He is not summoned."

"Then I will not answer," Holmes retorted, thrusting the paper back at him. "It is both or neither. And do not think you can drag me away," he added, when one of Brown's grizzled eyebrows rose. "You know who and what I am. I assure you I

100

am capable of making just the sort of scandal you have been ordered to avoid."

Brown's dark eyes shifted from Holmes to me, and for a moment he simply stroked his sandy beard. He was clearly uncomfortable, yet at the same time he was sharp and decisive. "Very well," he snapped. "Come then. 'Tis not on my head if she throws ye in the dungeon."

This did not sound promising, but Holmes was already plucking my overcoat from its peg and tossing it to me.

Outside, a dark carriage waited. I had barely time to register its crepe-covered sides, the way it was dressed as a hearse, before Brown had the door open and was shoving me inside. He mounted the driver's box and whipped up the horses.

"Holmes, what the devil is going on?" I demanded. Much to my surprise, my friend lifted a gloved finger to his lips.

"No conversation," he warned. "Brown's hearing is preternatural."

I understood at once; we were being spied upon. I nodded and settled back in my seat. I endeavoured to take in the details of our conveyance, but I was constantly frustrated. As my gaze would settle on some small part of the vehicle, a black fog would immediately cover that surface, giving every part of the carriage the appearance of being smudged or even erased.

We lurched to a stop and Brown opened the door, signalling for us to exit. Much to my astonishment, we were at Paddington Station. Like the carriage, it was wreathed in a strange fog, which allowed me only the briefest glimpse of the depot's sign before obscuring all the familiar objects of the great railway hub. Brown marched inside, forcing us into a smart canter to keep up with him. The platform seemed deserted, but as we approached its edge I saw a locomotive with a single car attached.

"A most unique special," Holmes said, into my ear. I boarded the conveyance reluctantly, for I had become convinced during our brief journey that Brown was taking us into hell itself. Instead, the train began to glide forward. I listened for the whistle, or the clacking of the wheels, yet heard nothing. We moved along silently, as if the train were skating down the tracks. Brown sat in the car with us, his dark and menacing gaze negating any thought of discussion. I tried looking out the window, but the thick fog made any impressions meaningless.

Perhaps an hour later---though that was only a guess on my part, for when I looked at my watch I noted that the hands had frozen---we arrived at another station. Once again Brown led us to a waiting carriage, and we took another short trip through a meaningless territory. The horses halted, and Brown opened the door.

Finally, the unnatural fog had lifted. I looked up at the familiar rounded walls of Windsor Castle.

"My word," I breathed, but Brown allowed me no time to gawk. He drew us through the Lower Ward to a side door, one that gave access to the famous Saint George's Chapel. We stood in the aisle, studying the magnificent heraldic carvings and the brightly hued banners. The interior of the sanctuary was illuminated by hundreds of flickering candles, as if readied for a royal service. It was easy to imagine the ghosts of great kings walking in procession down the aisle, surrounded by their stoutest knights. Generations of noble families seemed to stand invisibly at my elbows.

"Holmes," I whispered, struggling to find my voice, which seemed stolen by the sanctified splendour all around me. "Why have we been brought here?"

"Because, gentlemen, a crime has been committed." At the thin, imperious tone, we turned. John Brown re-emerged from an antechamber, leading a short and very stout woman. A long cloak covered her, but as she walked we saw the hint of lace and linen, the suggestion of a shift beneath the frayed velvet. She moved slowly, but with immense dignity.

The pair halted only a few paces before us. Small, chubby hands reached up to push back the hood.

Her Majesty Victoria, by the Grace of God Queen of the United Kingdom of Great Britain and Ireland, Defender of the Faith, and Empress of India, stood before us.

Chapter Fourteen

To my reader I will confess that I nearly lost all composure. It is one thing to see the Queen's picture in *The Times*, or to hail her from a distance as she passes in a parade, shielded by the glass and gilt of the royal carriage. It is another thing entirely to see one's beloved sovereign in her nightdress, with only a shabby cloak thrown over her. The Queen's long, uncoiled hair fell in a thin grey river over her shoulder. Her hands were plump and liver spotted, her fingers swollen around her wedding band and her ring of state. Tiny, much scuffed red velvet slippers were on her feet. For an instant she reminded me so much of Mrs. Hudson that I wondered, foolishly, if they might be kin. John Brown's loud cough reminded me forcefully of my place, and I dipped into the deepest bow I could manage.

"Ma'am," I murmured, "Your Highness."

Holmes executed a much more dignified obeisance. "Your Majesty," he whispered. "How may we serve you?"

She ordered us to both rise. Her face was soft but puckered, with tiny wrinkles at her mouth. The intensity of the light stripped her countenance of its regal nature, placing dark, exhausted circles beneath her eyes. She appeared all too frail and human. This was an elderly woman who stood before us, tired and almost at the end of her days.

And yet there was something about her that went beyond mere mortality. She radiated authority despite her sad condition. Her chin was raised and her eyes calm and calculating. I felt that I was being measured, summed up. The fingers that held my hat tightened until the bowler's brim was completely crushed. At last, she gave a tiny nod.

"It is acceptable to us," she said, with a short glance to her servant. "You did right to bring Doctor Watson as well."

"I---thank you, Your Majesty," I blurted, only to feel blood rise to my face as I realized that I had not been addressed. Holmes, however, had no fear of speaking first to his Queen.

"I take it some precious object has been stolen from the chapel?"

"Not a precious object, Mr. Holmes," she said, in a soft tone that could cause czars and potentates to tremble. "The precious object."

"Ah," he answered, "if I may be allowed to view the scene?"

She gave a tight nod and extended her hand to John Brown. He took it, leading her toward the altar. I presumed we were to follow. Holmes spoke lowly as we made our way up the narrow aisle.

"The Queen refers to the great relic of Windsor, the heart of Saint George, England's patron saint, encased in a golden monstrance encrusted with diamonds."

I felt appallingly ignorant, and my predicament no doubt was clear on my face. Holmes took pity on me, for once.

"The relic has not been displayed in our lifetimes, Watson, so do not feel alarmed that you have never heard of it. Even most professors of antiquities believe that it vanished during the upheavals of the Civil War."

"But why is it hidden?"

"For safety, Watson, though it now seems such a precaution was useless. No monarch since Charles II has felt that the great relic would survive if placed before the public. The temptation to desecrate it or to pluck the diamonds from its base would be too great to resist."

I considered what little I knew of relics. "Does it truly contain the heart of the saint?" I asked.

Holmes shrugged. "Considering how many femurs and phalanges and ribs of Saint George are venerated, across the continent, I find it doubtful that we could possess the actual vital organ of the dragon-slayer. But Sigismund, then King of the Romans and later Holy Roman Emperor, gave this relic to Henry V in 1416, when Sigismund was admitted to the Order of Saint George at Windsor Castle. It was most likely a bribe, to help secure the Treaty of Canterbury, but generations of

107

garter knights have bowed before it over the centuries." Holmes reached into his pocket and removed his magnifying glass. "A belief evolved around this particular relic, that if it were to go missing the monarch would no longer have the saint's protection, and England would be vulnerable to attack by dragons."

This was too much. "Dragons?" I hissed.

"Not in the form of fire-breathing monsters, Watson, but in the shapes of England's traditional enemies---the French, the Spanish, the Germans. Should the heart of Saint George be taken, our sovereign and our island would be imperilled."

We had reached the high altar. A number of jewelled chalices and candlesticks sat upon it, but they had not been disturbed. Instead, just behind the altar, the flagstones had been battered apart, revealing a small depression beneath. A shred of half-decayed cloth was all that was left in the hole. Holmes knelt, studying it closely.

"We were woken in the night, Mr. Holmes," the queen stated, "by the sense that something was amiss. I summoned Mr. Brown, and together we came down to the chapel and found the damage already done."

"There was no alarm raised?"

"No," she stated. "The guards have seen and heard nothing. There was only the missing heart---and that!"

Her disgust was such that she might have been pointing to a serpent, or some other loathsome reptile, in her chapel. Mr. Brown lifted a tartan shawl that covered an object some five feet away from the hole, in the shadow of a great crucifix.

It was a sword, its point battered and twisted, as if someone had flailed upon the floor with it. Holmes moved over and considered it carefully. The inference was obvious.

"This was used to loosen the flagstone and remove the monstrance from its niche. Watson, it looks familiar, does it not?"

Holmes held the damaged blade to me, and I took it with some reluctance, fearful of yet another enchantment or spell. I felt only the coldness of the steel, and the rough texture of the leather that was wrapped around the handle. Holmes drew my attention to the pommel, which bore a crest of a raven. Suddenly I recalled where I had seen this weapon. It had hung above a mantel at Whitborne House.

"Can you retrieve it, Mr. Holmes?" the Queen asked, as my friend pulled the shawl back over the sword. "Does this weapon give you any clues as to the culprit?"

"An essential one, Ma'am," he answered. "I have all hopes that I can restore the sacred object to its rightful place."

"Soon?" the Queen inquired, and for the first time I heard a tremble in her voice. Her hands clasped together, squeezing anxiously.

"As quickly as possible, Your Majesty."

She stared down at the dismal hole in the floor. "You have my license, Mr. Holmes. Do whatever is necessary to retrieve the heart of Saint George and the power of the Crown will stand behind you."

Holmes bowed again. John Brown took his Queen's hand, and I understood that the audience was over. Belatedly, I dipped down, listening intently as the Queen's nightgown made wispy noises across the floor.

"Holmes," I whispered, when mistress and servant were only distant shadows in the nave, "is the Queen a creature of the Shadows?"

"My word, what an idea!" Holmes scolded. "Of course not!"

"But her connection to the relic, to waken in the moment it was stolen?"

"Is explained by her royal blood, Watson. There is a sacred tie at work, a certain thread that binds our monarchs to the realm and all that is holy within it." He favoured me with an arch smile. "And tomorrow, she will rise from her bed with no memory of serving as our hostess or of giving me my marching orders."

"Good heavens, do you mean to tell me she was sleepwalking all this time?"

"Precisely."

"But the man, John Brown, is he---"

Holmes touched my arm. I turned, and saw Brown striding down the aisle. He looked furious, as if he might draw his dagger from his stocking and slice both our throats.

"Ye will come with me," he ordered, instead. Once again we were marched back to the waiting carriage, and returned on the silent, mystic train. At Paddington, another carriage stood at the ready. Dawn was just breaking when we were at last delivered back to Baker Street. "Ye will not speak of this," Brown ordered, in lieu of a farewell. He snapped the reins and the horses whinnied and bolted. The carriage turned in the street, and as it charged away from our doorstep I saw that what I had taken to be horses were instead equine skeletons with blazing eyes and fire spewing from their nostrils.

"Come inside," Holmes advised, tapping me on the shoulder.

Chapter Fifteen

I staggered through our doorway, feeling like a man entranced. We climbed the stairs to our sitting room, where Holmes stoked up the nearly defunct fire. As I warmed myself before it I once more found the courage to try to understand the bizarre, supernatural world I had fallen into.

"Holmes, that man, that John Brown---what was he?"

"A guardian spirit, Watson. A soul assigned to watch over the Queen and protect her."

"A heavenly spirit?" I asked, thinking it strange that the Lord of Creation would chose such an uncouth messenger. Holmes shook his head.

"A Shadows guardian, Watson. There are those within the Shadows who wish to maintain the balance, even as there are those who wish to destroy it. Some force from this netherworld has our Queen's, and therefore our nation's, interests at heart."

"But who?"

Holmes shrugged. "It hardly matters, Watson, though if I were to accept a wager, I would place my money on Boadicea, the warrior queen of the Britons. She is surprisingly sentimental on the subject of female rulers, despite being famous for her ferocity."

I decided to confine my inquiry to the matters at hand, to delve no deeper into the history of the Shadows. I felt overwhelmed and confused. Holmes' hand settled on my shoulder.

"Perhaps you should rest."

"Rest!" I protested. "When it seems that England is awash in thefts of sacred things? The bodies, the ravens, a magical rock and now a desiccated saint's heart? What will go missing next, Excalibur?"

Holmes' smile was grim. "It would not surprise me if it too has vanished, but fortunately that message has not yet arrived."

"But why?" I demanded. "It seems rather a bizarre collection of things for some criminal from the Shadows to steal."

Holmes returned to the table and considered the final note, which he had been unable to read before we were summoned to Windsor. With a grunt, he handed it to me. As he had predicted, it was a message from Inspector Lestrade, filled with remarkable invective against Holmes for his order to keep watch over Highgate. At times I did pity the poor man, so short on deductive gifts and so frequently and callously manipulated by Holmes.

"Let us see if Mrs. Hudson can provide some breakfast, and then we will review the facts at hand." Holmes rang the bell but I was certain that his sudden request for food was not related to his own hunger. He was a man who could go for days without subsistence when the working fit was on him; I could only assume that he was showing a rare regard for my welfare. Indeed, he took a terrible risk, for our good landlady was none too pleased with being awoken at such an indecently early hour, especially after being rousted at such an obscenely late one the night before.

While we awaited the arrival of provisions, Holmes dug about in the litter on the floor, the accumulation of old papers and journals, until he found the chalkboard that had more than once played a role in resolving a crime. He began to list the objects which had disappeared, noting each one's significance to the realm of either Sun or Shadows.

"It seems to me, Watson," he muttered, some time later, as we consumed our second pot of coffee, "that most of these objects are items which cross the threshold of the worlds. The London Stone is associated with an ancient, legendary king. The ravens are birds powerful and symbolic to forces of both darkness and light. The heart of Saint George channels the power of a saint who batted a monster of the Shadows; one might say that his battle is a symbol of a clash between the worlds. But the bodies…I confess, Watson, the stolen bodies of Highgate Cemetery baffle me. Why would anyone in the Shadows go to such trouble as to steal worthless corpses? "

"And Titania's crown?" I asked.

"Another most distracting anomaly, Watson. Unlike these other objects, it is an artefact from the Shadows, with no relevance to the world of Sun. I feel it must be connected, yet I lack the ability to explain why. It, like the bodies, is a thread that slithers from my grasp."

"Perhaps you would do better to approach the case from the opposite end," I said, grateful that the coffee was strong. "What did you learn from our visit to Whitborne House?" I asked as I handed my friend another cup.

"Distressingly little," Holmes harrumphed. "The old knight has been hexed; the son was perfectly within his rights to speak of his sire as spellbound. No offense to your skills as a physician, Watson, but his illness has no natural cause. I could feel the force of that spell pressing against my own senses, and I noted salt and chalk spilled across the threshold."

"Why did you not say anything when we were there?"

"I feared that if I made my knowledge plain, the magic-user within the dwelling would kill him. I deduced there was a reason why he was kept alive, and I did not wish to threaten that."

"Perhaps if we knew why he was allowed to survive then we might---" I began, only to cut short by a pointed cough from Holmes.

"We do know, Watson," he said, with a return of his former impatience. "We have since learned the reason. They needed him for their crime."

My confusion was surely plain on my face. Holmes rose to the chalkboard, resuming his lecture. "No matter how powerful a creature of the Shadows is, he can not profane a blessed sanctuary. For that, a Shadows being would need a mortal tool, one who could be spellbound to do the unholy work. You recall the crest upon the sword?"

"Yes. I saw it at Whitborne House."

"The Whitbornes are being used by the Shadows. One of them broke into Saint Swithin's Church and stole the London Stone, while the other was taken to Windsor and forced to unearth the heart of Saint George. The father is physically weak, unable to resist any unnatural force. The son perhaps could have struggled against the darkness, but he has been spellbound in his grief for his father and is thus unable to fight the creatures who work subtle magic against him."

I recalled a detail of our interview. "He knew nothing of the ravens being taken to the Tower."

"Yet if we were to demand the paperwork for the replacement ravens, we would no doubt find his signature upon the documents," Holmes sighed. He slumped into the basket chair and, for long moments, was lost in thought. Shamefully, and despite the infusion of several cups of strong coffee, I had just dozed off when his sharp question roused me.

"Watson, what was the servant called?"

I struggled to tease the name from my exhausted brain. "Samedi, I think."

"Yes---now I remember, I thought it odd that a Negro servant would bear such an unusual name. But Lady Whitborne was from America, late of the city of New Orleans, where such an exotic name would cause no raised eyebrows." Holmes rose and pulled another volume of the index from the shelf. He flipped through it rapidly, sending loose pages flying to the floor. He cursed and at length hurled the rest of the scrapbook down to join the scattered clippings. "There is a limit to even my knowledge, Watson, especially where it concerns the more primitive practices of our American cousins. I think a visit to the Library is necessary."

"The British Library?" I asked. "But surely it is too early for it to be open."

"I do not refer to that august institution," Holmes said, "but to one much more ancient and invisible. Into your coat and..."

He went still, and after a paralyzed instant slowly brought one finger to his lips. He edged to my side and leaned against me, slipping a request into my ear.

"Give me your revolver."

117

Without thought, I turned and retrieved it from my overcoat. He took it, secured a round into the chamber and, wordlessly, spun and delivered a shot through the window. The explosion and the shattering glass was enough to wake the proverbial dead. Holmes leapt over the chair and stuck his head through the new opening.

"Holmes, what was it?"

"A raven, Watson. We must hurry---I had hoped that by using an alias and not employing an excess of magic while on enemy territory I would remain invisible to our foes. But they are aware of me, and they know who and what I am. Our time is shorter than before, to prevent whatever chaos the forces of the Shadows have planned."

"So we must return to Whitborne House?"

"Yes, but not before we arm ourselves properly," he said, shoving the revolver back into my grasp. "To the Library, where the best weapons are forged."

Chapter Sixteen

"The fair sex is your department, Watson," Holmes said as we made our way toward a dreary corner of Whitechapel. "And I expect you to be your usual charming self. Play the part of the ardent swain and you will ably assist my efforts."

"Holmes, I hope you are not implying that I should woo one of these ladies," I complained, drawing further back into the confines of the hansom cab. While in my younger days I had occasionally known the charms of women of questionable virtue---as any army man might!---the prostitutes of London's lowest slum were barely recognizable as human beings. Most were old, all were dirty, and their wares, so crassly and vulgarly displayed, could be bought for next to nothing. I recalled how, a decade before, the mysterious figure known as Jack the Ripper had struck such terror and revulsion into all of London as he preyed upon these hideous and pitiful hags. The average Londoner, who assumed that sporting women must be beautiful, gay girls, had but to journey down Miller's Lane to learn the truth. These were women of both misfortune and debauchery, only a few short steps from the grave and damnation.

"No, Watson, the lady you are about to meet is far removed from these unfortunate femmes. She has tended to the Library of the Arcane since its conception."

"And when was that, Holmes?"

"In Egypt, during the reign of Alexander."

I had learned, at last, to stop objecting, to cease postulating the impossibility of the wondrous things Holmes told me. We disembarked, and I followed him into a pub called *The Quill and Scroll.* I had assumed such an establishment would be closed at this hour, but the pub was filled with odd types, its patrons bending over books as well as pints of frothy ale. Holmes spoke a few words to the man behind the counter, a swarthy fellow in a beard and turban, who gestured for us to part a beaded curtain in the rear of the establishment. We descended a number of darkened staircases, and I was reminded of the perilous depths of the *Bar of Gold,* that notorious opium den I had once ventured into on a mission to rescue a friend. The stairs kept taking us downward, far below the level of the underground rails.

"Holmes, is this library located in Hades?" I asked, as we made yet another turn, and this time found ourselves on a spiral brass stairway.

"On the contrary, Watson! To lovers of knowledge, it is paradise."

We had reached a threshold, a simple wooden door. Holmes knocked once. Without waiting for a response, he pushed it open.

I felt my jaw loosen, a rush of air stab my chest. We were entering a massive chamber, one that stretched further than the eye could see. It was illuminated with an unearthly, golden glow, yet no lamps or torches were visible. The walls were lined with books, charts, scrolls, and canisters of all descriptions. Angled shelves hinted that we were viewing only a foyer, and that far more wonders were hidden within.

I looked down and saw that the floor was made of solid gold.

"Doctor Watson, if you can tear your eyes away from the dream of King Midas," Holmes gently chided, tugging at my arm, "I give you the Lady Hypatia, the librarian of the Arcane and Guardian of all Immortal Knowledge."

I expected some bizarre creature, perhaps another fairy with wings or a witch with snakes growing from her skull. Instead, the woman Holmes presented to me was tall and willowy, with ginger hair in a prim bun and small spectacles atop her nose. She was dressed in what looked to be a nightgown, but on further inspection proved to be a kind of toga, with yards of gossamer thin cloth wrapped around her body. She peered at me with somewhat myopic green eyes and extended a slender hand, which I bent to kiss.

"Welcome, Doctor Watson. I have enjoyed reading your stories about my former pupil, though I suspect you make up the romance, as Master Sherlock was always keen to avoid even a hint of it even in his youth."

I was struck dumb by her words. Surely Holmes was the elder of the pair and yet he had claimed that her origin was in ancient Egypt. I struggled to be gallant, as Holmes had advised, to demur that the lady was too kind. It was then that my eyes fell back upon her little hand and I saw that it was riddled with scars.

"Ah—my dear, what…"

She pulled away, sighing at my look of astonishment. She tilted her head toward Holmes, who was already tearing books from a shelf. "You did not tell your friend about me?"

"There was not time."

"Sherlock!" she snapped, "You are as impudent as ever. Mycroft would never be so rude!" She rolled her eyes and removed her spectacles, tapping them in her palm. "Do forgive me, Doctor Watson, but your friend is as taxing a pupil as ever walked between the worlds."

I was still astounded by the brutality of the scars. And now, that I looked closer, I could see the white lines of them on her porcelain throat. More scars were woven like a braid along the length of her arms. Mercifully, her face had been spared, though small tendrils of the wounds peeked from her hairline. "He told me only that you once lived in Alexandria."

"Hundreds of years ago. I was a scholar and philosopher, the daughter of Theon, the last librarian of Alexander the Great's institution of learning, the place where all the knowledge of the civilized world was stored. But I angered the Christian archbishop Cyril by flaunting my intelligence, by taking on male students and refusing to marry and breed as he decreed a woman should. He roused the mob against me, and they attacked me as I rode in my chariot." Her expression made it clear these memories, though centuries old, were still vivid and painful to her. "They tore me apart with oyster shells."

"But then how...are you a ghost?" I whispered, such being the only conclusion that seemed logical.

"A ghost would not enjoy compliments," she said, with a flirtatious smirk. "Tell me that I am beautiful."

"Why, of course. You are very...ah...very lovely."

She laughed. "Surely you were more poetic when you wooed Mary Morstan, Doctor. But I will spare you further embarrassment and tell you that I was brought back from the dead by a magus of Osiris, who blotched the spell and cursed me with eternal life."

"But how could that be a curse?" I inquired. "To live forever would be a gift!"

"No, Doctor, you are wrong. It is the worst hell imaginable." She closed her eyes, and I began to comprehend her meaning. She was immortal but she was also human, so her attachments would be to humans. Over many centuries, she had surely watched friends and perhaps even lovers wither and die. I was swept with a feeling of great sympathy for her, as the tragic nature of her existence became clear to me. She drew a deep breath, opened her eyes, and gave me a warm smile, as if immediately dismissing any morbid thoughts. "But the occasional scholar like your friend Mr. Holmes makes it endurable." She turned, speaking to Holmes. "So what have you forgotten this time, Master Sherlock?"

He had climbed up onto a high ladder and was rapidly turning pages of an oversized textbook. "I have not forgotten anything. But I am concerned that I may have misplaced a memory."

"Semantics hardly impress a woman who debated with Plato's heirs. What are you looking for?"

"A reference to a figure known as Samedi."

Her thin body stiffened. "Is this figure of African extraction?"

"By way of America," Holmes answered, turning on the ladder. "You know him?"

"He is perhaps the one person of the Shadows I am least likely to encounter. Come down, that work on Cherokee mythology will not do you any good. Follow me."

We trailed her into the depths of the library, passing row upon row of books, artefacts, and relics kept inside cases of glass. From time to time I was so startled or so captivated by an object that Holmes was forced to grab me by my elbow and drag me along. At last Hypatia reached a door that was secured by a plethora of locks and chains. As she removed keys from a silver chatelaine, I nudged Holmes and inquired what manner of wild beast or dangerous spirit was confined inside the chamber.

"None, Watson. Only books. They are quite dangerous, these particular tomes, and have a bad habit of running away. Should they escape into the mortal realm, the mischief they could cause would be unspeakable."

Chapter Seventeen

The last chain fell from the door. I wondered if I should draw my gun, but Holmes only chuckled when I suggested it. Much to my horror, Hypatia entered the room alone, despite the ominous growls and moans that I could hear emanating from inside.

"Holmes!" I exclaimed, "We cannot allow her to go in there unprotected!"

My friend's amusement deepened. "Watson, we would be the ones endangered if we were to pass beyond that portal." As if to prove his words, the lady emerged a moment later. She passed a slender reference book to Holmes before turning and securing the bonds anew. Its title was written in a weird, spidery script, in a language unknown to me.

"*The Loa of the New World*," Holmes read, as fluidly as if the tome was composed in English. "A guide to the gods and spirits of the practitioners of voodoo." He glanced at me. "You have heard of this weird religion, Watson?"

"Only in most general terms," I confessed, as Holmes laid the book upon a nearby desk. The Lady Hypatia joined us, taking a seat and appearing to read the words upside down with ease. "It came to the United States with the slaves, did it not? And worshippers must offer bizarre sacrifices in order to obtain the favour of its deities?"

"An excellent summation, Doctor," Hypatia said, and I found myself beaming at her approval. "But only a very shallow one," she countered, and I began to sense where Holmes might have learned his trick of offering praise with one hand and a slap with the other. "Voodoo is more than some form of charm-magic or pagan superstition. It is a complex faith, a blending of pagan and Christian rites developed by a powerless people to help them take vengeance on their cruel masters. It is a crossroads, a place where the Shadows and the Sun are one, as the faith takes elements from both the darkness and the light."

"The loa are spirits in voodoo," Holmes said, running a lean finger down the page as if devouring the words by touch.

"More than mere spirits, they are aspects of the dark divine," Hypatia whispered. "The name you spoke, Samedi---it could be a reference to Baron Samedi, the voodoo lord of the dead."

Holmes snapped up. "Tell me."

"He is the one who gathers in the souls of the departed," Hypatia said, flipping the book's pages. She halted at an engraving of a bizarre character. "He is depicted as a tall black man, though sometimes his face is painted white, to resemble a skull. He wears a frock coat, a silk hat, and gloves. Wads of cotton are stuffed into his nostrils, as if he were a corpse prepared for burial."

I felt my blood freeze in my veins as I recalled the butler and his strange appearance. "Robert Whitborne said Samedi was Lady Ariel's servant."

Hypatia scowled. "The dread baron is no one's servant, though it was rumoured that certain voodoo kings and queens could summon him to do their bidding."

Holmes rose to his full height, folding his arms. I studied the book for myself, turning more pages. While I could not decipher the words, I could examine the illustrations of strange ceremonies conducted by dark-skinned voodoo initiates. A man held a rooster aloft, knife poised to slit the animal's throat. A woman in white danced with a large snake around her neck. But strangest of all was a drawing of men and women lurching forward toward a cowering overseer. Their arms were extended and their eyes were vacant, yet they were drawn up into ranks like soldiers.

"What are they?" I muttered, not aware that I had vocalized my thoughts. Holmes looked over my shoulder.

"Zombies," he said airily. "Animated corpses. Lacking their souls, they exist only as puppets to do the will of a powerful magician."

I nearly slammed the book shut, as it occurred to me that such might be my own fate, as I now lacked a soul. "Can they be stopped?" I asked.

"Only by fire or water, which purifies them of the evil animation," the lady librarian answered. "Decapitation will also destroy them, but otherwise sword and steel are no match, and bullets pass right through their bodies."

"One would need to be a very powerful magus to create such an infantry," Holmes pondered. "The book implies that they could be raised as an army of the dead. My lady, do you know of anyone from the Shadows who possesses such energy?"

"Not of the Shadows. It would need to be a Halfling like yourself, Master Sherlock, as the dark forces of the Shadows would be applied to the dead flesh of humans, who once existed in the Sun. Only half-breeds can use power in this manner."

I stared at my friend. "There are others like you?"

"That fact should be self-evident, my dear Watson--- you already know Mycroft. And did you think my mother was the only fairy foolish enough to lose her heart to a mortal?"

"The Halflings are more dangerous than either those born to Shadows or Sun," Hypatia said, with wariness to her words. "They are perpetual outcasts, always so very cunning and eager for power in the worlds that have rejected them. I hope you remember my warnings and my ethical teachings, Master Sherlock."

He nodded a dismissal to her concerns. "Let us remain focused. There must be some mastermind behind this plot. Who would have the strength to control such a forceful creature as Baron Samedi?"

"Lady Whitborne!" I exclaimed.

Holmes barely suppressed a groan. "But she's dead, Watson."

"No! Look!"

I jabbed my hand at an illustration. It showed a regal, honey-skinned woman of Creole descent, a six starred turban wrapped around her head. "Marie Laveau," Holmes read, "the voodoo queen of New Orleans."

"Holmes, I tell you, this is the same woman," I insisted. "Her photograph was in the store on Oxford Street, with the pictures of the celebrated beauties. Her etching was in every newspaper! Ariel Whitborne was an alias."

"If that is so, then you have entered the darkest and most dangerous waters imaginable," Hypatia said.

Holmes looked to his tutor. "What do you know of her?"

Hypatia reached her hand out toward the book, only to draw it away at the last second, as if the tome was a viper about to strike.

"Marie Laveau is a Halfling, and said to be the most powerful of the American witches. She adopted the role of a

130

voodoo priestess in order to tap the inherent magic in the great faith of its followers. She portrayed herself as a benefactor, a wise woman who told fortunes, lifted curses, and provided love potions; her supplicants loved her. In return, she thrived on their belief and grew ever more powerful from their worship of her."

Holmes arched an eyebrow. "According to this volume, she died in 1853."

"Who is to tell a voodoo queen, much less the greatest American practitioner of the evil arts, when to die?" Hypatia posed, over loosely woven fingers. "I would suggest an immediate telegram to the Chief of Police in New Orleans. I suspect that you will find an empty tomb at the end of it."

Holmes took the book from the desk and scanned down the passage. "If so, we face a very formable opponent, one able to feign her own death or to recover from it. But what would be her ultimate goal? What is the link between the bodies from Highgate Cemetery and the vanished relics of Britain's storied past?"

"Relics?" Hypatia asked. Holmes rapidly told her the rest of the tale, and though her expression showed distress, she also seemed removed, as if hearing of some distant relative's misfortune. At last she reached out and slipped the volume from Holmes' fingers. "To find the answer to this mystery, you will have to move beyond my sanctuary. Your answer is in a book not yet written."

Holmes smiled, took her hand and kissed it. "We can not tempt you into duty?"

"I have no desire to see anything of this modern world. A century that decrees such infernal bondage for females as corsets and bustles is not for me. However, we have not yet discussed the price for the information and tutorage I have provided."

"You can't give her my soul," I grumbled, when Holmes looked at me with some speculation, "Titania already has it. And no one in their right mind would want yours."

Holmes laughed heartily. "You've developed a somewhat pawky sense of humour, my dear fellow!"

Hypatia intervened in our baiting. "Doctor Watson, if you will merely promise me a copy of whatever memoir this adventure produces, I will count honour satisfied."

"You will have it, dear lady," I pledged, even as Holmes turned and hurried for the door, "if only I survive to write it."

Chapter Eighteen

I have but vague recollections of our ride back from Whitechapel. Holmes stopped once to send telegrams, again without mentioning their destinations. He had become obsessed with finding the connection between the various threads he now held in his hand, in order to weave them into a comprehensible tapestry of a case. I quickly deduced, in the interim, that my conversation was unwanted and, lacking Holmes' superhuman abilities to remain awake for unnatural amounts of time, I availed myself to the opportunity to rest. While Holmes paced around the sitting room, turning the air purplish black with the smoke from his pipe, I dropped off on the sofa. I awakened only when Holmes smacked my feet to the floor and announced we had company for luncheon.

Our guest was none other than Inspector Lestrade. I have given my readers many pictures of him throughout the narratives of my adventures with Sherlock Holmes. Let me add only that I had never seen him looking more nervous and ferret-like than at that moment. His beady eyes darted around the rooms and he tore into the biscuits like a famished animal.

"I don't know what kind of business this is, Holmes, but you've bloody well got every man at the Yard ordered to your beck and call. It was one thing when you told me to post extra constables at the cemetery---I'm glad to do it for you, though I'd appreciate a bit more warning in the future!---but you must simply call off the hounds of Whitehall. I've been dragged before more brass in the last day than a conductor in a sousaphone orchestra! 'What do you make of it, Inspector?' 'What does it mean, Inspector?' 'Why is the Home Secretary asking questions, Inspector?' 'Holmes is your friend, Inspector, what is he up to?' Do you realize what a fool I look like when I have to confess that I haven't the foggiest notion of what you're about?"

"Have some jam with your biscuit, Lestrade."

"Hang your jam! Out with it, Holmes, why is the Privy Council suddenly wanting constant dispatches from the Yard? And how does this tie in with that awful body-snatching of a few days ago? That's the only crime I know of!"

"Lestrade, you must have patience," Holmes advised. "If I could share my progress with you, I would. However, I fear that state secrets are involved."

The policeman's moustache quivered. "Are you being honest with me, Holmes?"

"As best I can, Inspector."

He huffed, shoved the rest of our meal into his pocket, and marched out the door without wishing us a good day. Holmes sighed and poured himself another cup of tea.

"It does distress me to use the man that way. Despite his total lack of intelligence or reasoning abilities, he has the loyalty and tenacity of a bulldog. I do not willingly abuse him."

"Ha! Confess your own faults, Sherlock, you enjoy baiting him as much as a matador savers the onrush of the bull."

My teacup went flying. I spun around, seeking the source of that full, deep voice, which could belong only to Holmes' elder brother, Mycroft. As the man was both tall and obese, it seemed highly unlikely that he could be secreted anywhere around our messy room. Holmes sighed and waved for me to stay in my chair. He stepped into his own room, and returned a minute later bearing his long mirror in its oaken frame.

His sibling appeared within the glass.

"That is much better. Greetings, Doctor Watson. As you know, I dislike leaving my rooms for any trifling matter, and I much prefer this form of communication. It is less taxing than even a hansom ride."

I merely sat with my jaw open, a posture I had adopted far too many times in the last few days. Mycroft chuckled.

"I am surprised at you, brother. When I received the telegram informing me that you had made your partner in crime aware of your true origin, it seemed most unlike your character to do so."

"These are special circumstances," Holmes defended.

"Ah---our aunt Titania has you somehow beholden to her again. No, do not attempt to explain," he said, with a motion of his flipper-like hand. "Merely bring me up to speed. I am certain that you will require my assistance whether you have the good grace to ask for it or not."

Holmes turned his back on the image, flashing a look of exasperation to me. However, he took a deep breath and began a concise recitation of the events, concluding with the visit from Lestrade. Mycroft settled into an armchair that had appeared from the scenery of a gentleman's study behind him, and occasionally interrupted the narrative to pose a pointed question or ask for clarification.

"It is a bid for power, brother. That much should be obvious."

"Of course it is! I am not a dunce, Mycroft. But how do they seek to achieve it? What is the method? I can find no precedent in either the world of Shadows or Sun."

"Perhaps it is some new technique."

"Ridiculous. Both of us know there is no such thing. Nothing new has ever been tried, especially not by the denizens of the Shadows." Holmes shook his head. "And it can not be a quest for power in the realm of Sun. They have never manifested such a keen interest in a place they consider inferior."

"Ah, but we no longer live in a world without allure to them," Mycroft countered, sounding much like a disappointed schoolmaster with an errant pupil. "The realm of Sun now has its own form of magic. Consider what steam and electricity are like to a common man. Any form of technology is, to a simpleton, a work of conjuring." Mycroft waggled a finger. "Perhaps these intriguers have found a way to take magic from both worlds, for some purpose you have yet to understand."

Holmes' face showed his astonishment with such a suggestion. "You propose that Marie Laveau and her paramour are somehow harnessing the realm of Sun to fuel their Shadows-based magic?"

"Is not that the ultimate fate, Sherlock? And if they succeed the human world is doomed," Mycroft said, as calmly as if he had just placed the order for his afternoon tea. "The world of Shadows will devour the world of Sun upon its own platter."

"It would be the end of days," Holmes whispered, sinking upon the sofa with his head in his hands. "The human world overrun by Shadows."

"No!" I shouted, startled by my own passion, yet thrilled with almost choking horror at the thought. "The Shadows can not win! Mankind is not destined to live in a world of darkness and never-ending fear."

Mycroft rumbled a chuckle. "Ah, now I see why my sibling retains you, Watson. You possess the optimism that he has long since lost." The stout man tilted his head. He seemed to peer right through me, to where his brother sat. "Their time is passing, Sherlock. Man has seen his last hour upon the stage. We are fortunate to have a choice, one that it is not too late for you to make, even though you have turned your back on our mother's world for so long now."

"As have you," I said to Mycroft, with some spirit.

"Do you think so, Doctor? How little you know me," Mycroft replied, and I heard beneath his words a great emptiness, a dark pit, as if he—instead of I—was missing a soul. "I have always looked to my own interests, my own pleasures. While they lasted in the human world of Sun I would take them, but when they are gone, I will not miss them. I may not be the magician that my brother is, but I know that I am far less idealistic and vastly more intelligent."

I was poised to make some objection when I heard Holmes speak my name. Mycroft abruptly vanished. I found myself glaring at my own reflection.

"He was of no help to you," I snorted.

"On the contrary, Watson," Holmes said, "he has forced me to the conclusion I did not want to draw. Our enemies are tapping the power of both worlds, with, it appears, the goal of destroying this one. And until I can see clearly how they are doing it, I have no strategy for how to fight them. Now let me sit quietly and attempt to think this through."

I nodded and returned to the table. Holmes stretched out upon the sofa, and I would have thought him asleep except for an occasional mumbled word, a half-formed sentence. At points he rose and lit his pipe, and before the afternoon was done the room was once again polluted with foul smoke. I perused the newspapers, finding the articles prosaic and mundane. A war was threatening in Asia, an epidemic was raging in Africa, and an election was looming in America, and yet these things now seemed small and unimportant. Then a notice in the local police report leapt out at me.

"Holmes! Do you recall the name upon the goldsmith's wagon?"

He grunted. "It was Mandel. Why?"

"Because his wife has advertised for news about him. It seems that he has been missing for the last three days."

Holmes instructed me to read the statement. It offered little information, only that one Geoffrey Mandel, a goldsmith and jeweller of Oxford Street, had left for work three days before and never returned home. His assistants stated that he had received a telegram and ordered them to close up the shop immediately, then dismissed them with a full day's pay for a mere hour's work. There was some speculation that Mandel was planning to entertain an illustrious client and did not want his helpers to know the client's identity. His wife claimed that he had never been so much as late for dinner in the past. Foul play was now suspected and anyone with information was urged to report to Inspector Gregson of Scotland Yard.

"Another link in our chain, Watson, and yet I fail to grasp it, to see what kind of monster writhes at the end of it!"

Holmes barely touched the excellent dinner that Mrs. Hudson brought to us at sundown. A short time later, a telegram and a written note arrived simultaneously. Holmes tore the first one open and gave a growl of approval.

"Just as the Lady Hypatia said, Watson! My correspondent is the head of the New Orleans police, who writes *'Laveau tomb opened, body removed, how did you know?'*"

I shivered at the confirmation that a notorious practitioner of dark arts was indeed alive and walking among us, and that she had married into one of the finest families in England without anyone being aware of her unseemly origins. "And the other?" I asked.

Holmes' face turned pale. He slid the paper to me.

Our friend the ravenmaster had been found inside the raven's cage, murdered, his eyes and flesh pecked apart by the vicious imposter birds.

"See what happens when my mind does not obey me, Watson? A good man's life snuffed out, and only the first of many unless I can piece together this mystery." He walked back to the sofa, dropping upon it listlessly. "Perhaps I would have done better to stay with the cocaine."

"Holmes, you can not mean that," I scolded.

" I think I do, Watson. You could not have known the real reason why I took that repulsive drug."

"I assumed it was out of boredom, a cure for ennui. Or to savour its momentary satisfaction."

"It was to dampen the magic. To live in the human world, I must constantly keep the magic that is instinct to me, like breathing, under heavy suppression. I must cage it, lest I give myself away as a Halfling. And the drug was successful, a precise means of dampening the magic, even if it wrecked havoc on my body. It had the bizarre effect of calming my mind, soothing me against the innate resistance to an unnatural life. Without it," he murmured, wiping sweat from his face, "my mind races, burns, tears me apart."

"Your mind is like some great engine," I said. "It is only to be expected that you would need to give it fuel."

"Yes, like some...." He lifted his head slowly, and I saw new light shine from his eyes. He made a startled cry and was suddenly on his feet. "Watson! You---you have given me the answer!"

"I have?" I asked, recalling my own words and finding nothing useful within them. Holmes was running about the room, retrieving objects from the table and the mantel, stuffing jars and bottles into his pockets. "What did I say?"

"The engine! That is what they are building, Watson, a vast and terrible *machine* that will take the elemental energy within those relics and focus it to rip down the veil between the worlds. Once that is done, an army of the dead will march through, followed by every cursed thing that lives in Shadows. My God, man, to think I almost did not see it in time!"

"But you can defeat them?"

"No, I can not, not alone. But *we* can, Watson. Together, we can throw a wrench in their engine and send the miserable Shadow beings back into the abyss where they belong. Come, into your coat, Watson. The game is afoot!"

Chapter Nineteen

"Faith, Watson, is the greatest source of power that any world can know," my friend said, as we both lay on our stomachs on a small ridge overlooking Whitborne House. Holmes had a pair of field glasses pressed to his eyes and was lecturing me as sedately as if we were nothing more than two bird watchers, hoping to catch a robin's flight upon a moor. "Think of the intensity of Christian believers at their prayers, or pagan devotees offering sacrifices to their wooden idols. Among certain tribesmen of the jungle, if one is told that the shaman or witch doctor has cursed him, it requires only a week before he is deceased. He looks to be hale and healthy, he eats and exercises, and yet he falls dead at exactly the hour decreed because he believes he will die."

"And this is the force that Marie Laveau wishes to use?"

"Exactly, Watson, and I was a fool for not envisioning it from the start. Had I merely put myself in her place, directing my own thoughts into evil passageways, I would have ultimately arrived at the same destination and methodology. It is a technique I have often applied in solving ordinary robberies. To catch a thief one must envision himself a thief. To fight the Shadows, one must be of the Shadows."

"I think I would find you a much less agreeable companion if you engaged in that practice too frequently, Holmes."

He cracked a laugh. "Ah, Watson, if you only knew the temptations for…there! Look closely and tell me what you see."

I took the glasses, quickly adjusting them to my vision. "The house is completely illuminated! It is brilliant."

"Indeed, it is a rather bright home for such a late evening as this, in a place so far removed from any regulated source of electricity. One wonders what is generating such powerful light; how ironic that it should come from the Shadows! Now direct your gaze to the top floor in the centre of the building, where Sir James' room is located. What do you see?"

"It alone is dark."

"I fear we may be too late to assist the poor fellow. His death will be on my head, Watson."

"Holmes," I argued, not for the first time, "would it not have been better to bring some of the regular police forces with you? Or even to call upon royal troops? You have carte blanche from the Queen herself."

"I can not risk their lives for a cause I could not explain. Besides, the element of surprise is on our side. Our enemies believe we are wandering the streets of London."

I nodded, still amazed by the phantoms Holmes had created to replace us and serve as a distraction to the watchers who, he was certain, followed our every move. He had taken a clipping of his own hair, mixed it with shag tobacco, and cast up the smoke from a pipe. Then with arcane words he shaped it until it was a passable facsimile of himself, from shined shoes to deep set eyes. Only upon drawing so close I could touch it did I see through the image, realize it was made of vapours. He created a second mannequin that bore my features, and sent both away. They moved as we did, walking out together side by side, like oldest friends. Neither spoke, but otherwise the imitation of life was complete. Watching around the drapes, we saw a raven depart from a lamppost opposite our door, flying after the illusions made of hair and smoke.

"How long will our twins walk the London streets?" I asked.

"Until dawn. It is possible that our spy might grow wise to the game, but ravens—even enchanted ones—possess only limited intelligence, and next to no imagination."

Now, overlooking our enemy's stronghold, I found Holmes' reassurance heartening. "So what is our plan?"

"No creature of the Shadows who wishes to work evil on this world will do so before the stroke of midnight. The wee hours, from twelve until three are the vulnerable time, when the veil between the worlds is at its thinnest. That gives us an hour to act before they do." He pulled me back behind the crest of the hill, whispered another of his magic words, and suddenly a replica of the house was laid upon his palm. It glittered with the same golden light that his familiar had cast. "The machine must be pointed east, toward the rising Sun. It is logical to assume that it rests somewhere amid the repairs of the eastern side of the building, perhaps behind double doors that could easily be opened and closed. The machine will also be heavily defended. The entire western side of the mansion has, I suspect, been given over to shelter the bones and corpses of Highgate."

"Thus the stench the workmen reported."

Holmes agreed. "It did not initially occur to our miscreants to cover their traces, but a simple spell, cast perhaps by Laveau herself, soon dulled the worker's senses, and ours. We smelled nothing."

An owl called in the distance. Holmes was quiet for a moment, waiting until the grounds were once again silent before renewing his discussion.

"If I read their scheme correctly, tonight they will fire up the machine, channel its energy into blasting a great fissure between the Shadows and the Sun, between the realities of the darkness and the light. As it opens, Laveau and Samedi will send their zombie minions out, to create panic and disorder. You recall Hypatia's words as to what will destroy them?"

"They can only be killed by fire or water."

"Or by beheading," Holmes said. "Their losses may be fantastic, but Laveau can create new zombies instantly from the many thousands of remains removed from Highgate. She will have ever more potential zombies from the bodies of those who are first slain. The zombies will be followed by creatures from the Shadows, monstrous beings summoned by Laveau's spells. It will only be a matter of time before she rules Britain, and then she will transport her great machine around the world. More rifts will open, more armies will be dispatched and it will be the end of days."

"Holmes, what does this machine look like?"

"I do not know. It will barely be recognizable as an engine, not to a man accustomed to the forces of steel and steam. The relics will be held within it, connected by gold, the purest, strongest, and surest conductor of power. Think of all the years of belief that have been absorbed in those items, Watson. The force of Britons believing in stone and birds and sacred hearts, objects on which the strength of the empire was based. Centuries of veneration and tradition will be harnessed, and once that machine is activated, there is no turning back."

"The supply of power is inexhaustible?"

Holmes frowned. "In theory, no. Had I time, there are certain calculations I could make to predict how long the infernal machine could run. Unfortunately, we have not a minute to spare."

"Then our first duty must be to destroy it. Wrench it apart."

"You are the express train of thought tonight, old friend. That is indeed the only appropriate opening move. Once the engine is gone, I believe that I can deal with Laveau and her ilk separately."

"With your magic?"

He inclined his head in answer. "Yes, though I would prefer bullets or the sword, Watson. I hope you will believe me in this regard."

"Of course I do. But why should the use of your magic be unwelcome to you?"

"Because until now you have only seen the lovely, reflective surface of it: the use of a familiar, the casting of an illusion, the ability to cloud a mind. If and when you witness the full force of it, you may see in me a man you do not wish to know."

I scoffed. "That would be impossible, Holmes."

His lips twitched, as if he wished to smile but had forgotten how. "Watson, my brother erred. It is not your optimism that makes you invaluable, it is your unwavering loyalty. I would be lost without you."

"Pshhh. You're talking nonsense," I said, even as I felt a warm rush of pride colour my cheeks. "Now, how will we get into the house without being seen?"

And so it was, five minutes later, I found myself boldly approaching the front door of Whitborne House, that very portal through which we had been so ungraciously ejected just a short time before. My job, as Holmes had explained it, was to cause a distraction. I was to be loud and abusive, to act like a drunken traveller who had stumbled upon the manor and sought refuge within. It was a foolhardy strategy for surely the residents (among them, by Holmes' reckoning, not only the voodoo queen and her consort, but the Morrigan of the ravens and Spring Heeled Jack, that devilish trickster who had aided Laveau's escape from her Highgate tomb, and an unknown number of zombies) would be on their guard against just such an interloper. I had no hope that I could lure them away from their dark experiment for any length of time.

But I did have a ring on my finger, situated where I had once worn my wedding band. Holmes had assured me that all I had to do was twist it, and I would instantly become invisible to all the Shadows' minions. I only needed to buy him a quarter hour, or even ten minutes, enough time to find a way through the household's defences and destroy the machine.

Once invisible, I was to race to the eastern wall, in hopes of rejoining Holmes and assisting his efforts.

It was not, I hasten to add, a plan that I had readily agreed to. It seemed to me that we would do better to present a united front. In this, Holmes was unshakable. He had to go alone. He insisted that my presence would only slow him down.

"Unaccompanied, I can walk through a wall, Watson. There are more steps to the spell if you are along, more chances my presence will be detected. Just do as I ask, and all will be well. They can not harm what they can not see."

But they could see me now. I confess that a tide of nervous sweat was dampening my shirt as I came onto the drive and approached the large fountain that fronted the door. I had ruffled my hair, undone my collar, and even taken a fortifying swallow from the flask of medicinal brandy that I always carried upon my person. I launched into a song from the days in the barracks, pitching my voice to an intoxicated tenor. I bid my sweet Jenny girl goodbye, rolling my lyrics with a Scottish brogue. I saw a window open, so I increased my volume and shouted out that an old soldier of an Indian regiment sought a bunk for the night. I swayed forward, banging on the door.

There was no answer.

I began to curse, my words growing ever more profane as I demanded entrance. I abused the residents as cowards, misers, and even Frenchmen. I staggered back, gasping for air and trying to think of some particularly insulting oath. Just then something tugged at my ankle.

I looked down to find that a species of moist vine had ensnared my leg. I wondered how it had managed to twist so tightly around my limb. Keeping up the invective, I crouched to pull it free.

It snapped and I was jerked sideways. The manor house spun, the sky was replaced overhead by the soil. The bright moon was somewhere above my feet.

I was being held aloft by a great vine! The monstrous tendril of a huge, red flowered plant had sprung from the filthy waters of the ornamental fountain. It swung me to and fro, like a child playing with a doll. I was screaming, my ears filled with my own terror, yet somehow beneath it all I heard laughter, as if my horrific plight was a comedy played upon a music hall stage. I tried to call for help, but blood rushed to my head and I began to feel faint.

The swaying ceased. I found myself suspended directly above the flower, which was larger in diameter than my own bed. Its red blossoms unfurled, revealing not the soft centre of a tender bud, but the sharp teeth and ravenous maw of some hellish beast.

The vines that supported me uncoiled, and I fell.

Chapter Twenty

I hit the water face first, causing a tremendous splash. By some miracle, the fountain was much deeper than it appeared, and my neck was not instantly broken, though a kind of shock rang through my entire frame. There was a long moment where time was suspended, and I floated through a wet darkness uncertain if I was alive or dead, merely half-conscious and unable to move my limbs. At last the need for air became urgent and my legs recalled how to work in unison, to kick and thrust and propel me back to the surface of the pool. I broke the water, gasping and wiping hair from my face, desperately seeking the location of the monster that had nearly devoured me.

The huge plant was laid across the rim of the fountain. To my astonishment, it was turning brown, its leaves curling up and crumbling as if deprived of liquid. The red blossom was fading, already coated with black spots along the edges. A foul odour, like carrion, was being emitted from the plant's body, the stench emerging in an audible hiss. I gagged and tried to pull myself out of the fountain, but it was impossible to get an adequate grip on the slime-covered walls.

"Let me help you."

I nearly lost my hold and sank back into the pool when I saw who stood over me. It was not one of the Shadows' creatures, nor was it Holmes, already returned from his task. To my astonishment, it was the Lady Hypatia, barely recognizable in new attire. She was dressed like an adventurer on safari, in jodhpurs and high boots, with a khaki jacket over a simple white blouse. Her hair was pulled in a long, loose braid, and as she held one hand out to me the other was jamming a large machete-style knife back into a sheath on her narrow waist.

"It'd say it was time to trim the shrubbery, wouldn't you?" she asked, with a wink. I took her offered hand, though it seemed impossible that such a slender woman could hoist me from the depths of the pool. By bracing a foot on a stone, I was able to assist, and between us we struggled until I was once again on dry land.

"My lady what...how...what was that thing?"

"That, my dear Doctor, was a species of Nile lotus mated with a crocodile, created to serve as a kind of watchdog for this house. It is a distressingly common practice in the Shadows, to place unnatural beasts upon a threshold. I shudder to think how many vagrants or peddlers have fallen into its maw in the past few days."

"But how did you come here? You said you would not leave the Library."

"I've made a discovery that Holmes must be informed of," she replied. Before she could elaborate, the door to the

154

manor house opened. She looked to it, then back to me. Pain clouded her delicate features. "Oh, Doctor, please try to forgive me."

"For what?" I asked.

The next second, I knew. Her scar-covered right fist crashed into my jaw, so unexpected and sharp that I was once more knocked off my feet, cowering on the hard gravel. Before I could rise, two figures had raced out and taken me roughly by the elbows.

To my further astonishment, they proved to be the Whitbornes, father and son. The old man was still withered and aged, clad only in his pyjamas, but he possessed unnatural strength. The son's eyes were vacant and a blue foam escaped his lips. Both were under some diabolical mental control, for my shouts and cries, my pleas for reason, went unheard. Instead they twisted my wrists and forced me to march behind Hypatia, who was setting a course for the interior of the house.

"Come in, come in!" a high-pitched voice called from the darkness. "A pretty girl and a foolish man! Fun, fun!"

I was unceremoniously escorted to what had once been a nobleman's dining hall. The long tables and chairs remained, and on the dais sat a bizarre figure. He was dressed as a cavalryman, with boots and spurs and close-fitted tunic, all in spotless white, but his skin was a devil's red while his goatee and slicked hair were midnight black. Four tiny horns protruded from his brow. When he clapped his hands together I saw that his nails were silver spikes. He gave a laugh, followed by a belch, and sulphurous fire spat from his lips.

"Greetings, Spring Heeled Jack," Hypatia said pleasantly. "I take it you are the doorman for this household?"

He laughed again and pulled his legs beneath him. He began to jump, up and down, higher and higher, as if the seat of the chair was a trampoline.

"A doorman? No, tsk, tsk, I will be a lord, a great ruler! I'll have all the pretty ladies I want to kiss and plenty of foolish men to scare in the night-time."

"And that is your only ambition?" Hypatia asked. "To molest and to frighten?"

"What more is there?" he asked, leaping down from the platform but continuing to bound around the room, literally bouncing off the walls like some kind of rubber ball. He turned somersaults and touched his toes. His body spun in midair. It would have been a delightful performance, one I might have laughed at, had it not been for the bone crushing pressure that the Whitbornes were applying to my arms, along with the sick apprehension that Holmes had misjudged his old tutor. Was she in league with these scoundrels and about to give us both over to them? "What more, what more?" the demon cried.

Hypatia's smile was arch. "Nothing, Jack. It is delightful to meet a man who knows the limits of his own ambitions."

It was Holmes' sardonic tone I now heard. I stared at the woman who was both my rescuer and betrayer, uncertain of what game was being played.

"Let me go!" I shouted, casting my lot. "I've done nothing! I'm just a traveller in the night."

"Silly man, silly man," Jack decreed. He turned a flip and landed nose to nose with me. His eyes were red spirals, swirling and casting off sparks like a Saint Catherine's wheel. I wiggled back as best I could, certain that he would incinerate me with a breath. "I will scare you over and over again, for all eternity! BOO!"

I futilely tried to pull away. I felt the skin on my left ear crackle and blister, as if pushed against a hot iron. Jack shrieked in merriment, executed a backward handstand, and pulled himself up before Hypatia.

"Fun, fun!"

"Now aren't you glad I saved him from your mistress' little pet?" Hypatia inquired, tickling beneath Jack's chin with one finger. "Where is the great queen? I have a gift for her."

"Busy now, she's very busy. Build the engine, all goes boom!"

My chest constricted as I realized that Holmes had miscalculated. The evildoers were not gathered together, making some council or war or feasting before their attack, but were even now working their twisted magic. He could be walking into a perfectly laid trap!

"They will find it impossible to turn their engine on without a key," Hypatia warned. Her message, or perhaps its tone, halted Spring Heeled Jack in mid-cackle.

"Without what?"

"Even you know the power of words, Jack. No spell can be activated without exactly the right word. And your mistress' great machine, which harnesses the force of faith, can not be engaged without the perfect word." She shook her head, and Jack frowned at her. Even though she was speaking clearly, he still seemed confused. "Jack, your queen needs a word from the greatest magus who ever lived and walked between the worlds." She reached inside her jacket and withdrew a small notebook. It was bound in leather, its covers tied together with many strings. "This is the spell book of Doctor Faustus. Your queen must consult it, if she wishes her engine to be anything more than an expensive toy. You sense this book's power---I can tell by your ears, the way they flatten against your head."

"Let me see it!" the imp demanded.

"Jack, you are a mere creature of the Shadows, not a wizard powerful enough to command them. This spell book would burn you straight into hell."

He whimpered. "But how do I know you tell the truth? Queen Marie punishes me. She does not like interruptions!"

"Fair enough," Hypatia allowed. "To demonstrate my veracity I will permit you one page." She undid the ties, looked through the volume and carefully removed a single sheet of vellum. "This is a simple spell that should put more spring in your step. Go on," she coaxed, as his clawed fists trembled. "Try it. You have nothing to fear."

He shook, as if feeling some terrifying power emitting from the small book, but at last a kind of bestial greed swarmed across his features and he grabbed the page. He read allow in a high-pitched voice, sometimes stumbling over words that were complete gibberish to me. He grew more excited with every passage, jumping up and down, a demon child with a new plaything. I sensed he was reaching some finale. With a crescendo shout of triumph he proclaimed the last word, twirling up into the air-.

-And bursting apart in a spray of red and golden fire, exploding across the ceiling like a living roman candle. Tiny pieces of him drifted down, flaming out as they hit the floor. The spellbound men behind me had no reaction to this wondrous yet horrifying display. Hypatia merely nodded.

"Spring Heeled Jack was as stupid as he was evil. Would that they were all that way." She turned and drew the machete from her belt. Though it pains me to confess it, I cursed at her.

"What in hell do you intend, Madame?"

"To release you from these enchanted servants, Doctor Watson. You do wish to be released, do you not?"

"Whose side are you on?" I demanded.

"Sherlock's," she promised. "I am sorry, but I had no time to explain. Spring Heeled Jack was the first obstacle. I knew he could be easily defeated, but now we have a more important task, you and I. We must get to that machine before my former pupil makes a terrible error."

"And what is that?"

She did not answer, but instead raised the machete as if to strike off the old knight's head. I gave another cry of protest.

"You can't!"

"Doctor, they are under the control of our enemies. I can not order them to release you."

"Why not? If you are a magician can you not bend them to your will?"

She made a bitter laugh. "I am a librarian, Doctor, and a passable mathematician. I could study magic for all my eternal life and never be able to use it myself. I can only assist others who seek to develop their gifts through study. That is why I had to devise a way for Spring Heeled Jack to murder himself. Now hush and let me---"

"No!"

"Doctor!"

"You can't kill him, or maim him." Both men stood still as statues, frozen to their work. My struggles were entirely futile. "There must be some other way."

"I am open to suggestions," she noted, in that same irritable tone that Holmes so often employed with me. A ginger brow arched. "Or I could just leave you behind."

"What does brandy do to the spellbound?" I asked.

"Brandy? You mean alcohol? Why…that's quite clever, Doctor Watson! I will only need to find some."

"In my pocket," I directed, and there was a bit of embarrassment when I had to redirect her from my jacket to my trousers. She merely smiled at me.

"When I was young, men wore no covering on their legs. That made hiding brandy flasks much more difficult."

She opened the silver container, moved to the old man's side, and forced the flask to his lips. He made a gurgling protest, but within seconds his hold on me relaxed. He crumpled to the ground, and moments later his burly son did the same. I knelt beside them, quickly taking each man's pulse.

"They are only asleep," Hypatia said, restoring the flask to me, "and when they awaken, the spell will be broken." She ripped another page from the book, pulled a pencil from her pocket and scribbled on it. "Place this message in the youngster's hand. Let us hope he will have the good sense to heed it."

Written on the page was *'For The Love Of God, Run.'*

I nodded my agreement and plucked my revolver from my jacket. "Now we can find Holmes."

"I have a better idea," she said, as we peered around a door, checking the hallway. Two miserable, stinking zombies stood just outside. We drew back, keeping our conversation to whispers. "Let them take us to him."

"What? Are you suggesting that we allow ourselves to be captured?"

"It is the surest way to get an audience with Laveau and her entourage," Hypatia said. "The American witch needs me for their work. Before the hour grows later, and her innate powers stronger, we must force her hand."

"No, I won't allow it."

"Very well, you stay here or…good heavens, is that an invisibility ring I see on your finger?"

I had forgotten about it, a fact that caused me a second wave of embarrassment. "It is."

"Clever Sherlock, to give you that! Very well then, use it, and follow. But we must move quickly."

"Dear lady, I will not stand to see---wait!"

My restraining motion was one second too slow. Hypatia stepped through the doorway, raising her hands and calling to the shrouded figures.

"Zombies, are you not? I surrender! Please, I beg you...don't hurt me!"

The creatures shuffled toward her, moaning and making incomprehensible grunts. I caught only a glimpse of their faces, but I saw corruption and decay marring their features. One of the pair was lacking his jaw, the other his eyes. Their clothes hung on them in tatters. It was a horror that should have made even a strong woman swoon. Hypatia simply gave herself over to them, with only a slight curling of her lip indicating her distain for the monsters. They pulled her along the hall, a foul door of rotting flesh in their wake.

Twisting the ring and trusting in my friend's magical arts, I trailed silently behind.

Chapter Twenty-one

Just as Holmes had predicted, the entire eastern wing of the house had been remodelled, the rooms and halls broken apart, creating one vast, three story high chamber that gave the impression of a great warehouse or barn. I slipped through the door behind Hypatia and the zombies. Spotting a ladder that led to a metal catwalk along the south side of the structure, I quickly scaled it. Thus I had a complete view of the bizarre tableau below me.

When Holmes had spoken of an engine, I had envisioned some great steam turbine, or even a loom from one of our northern factories. Instead, below me stretched a large web, its threads made of long golden cords. At two corners of the web were stolen artefacts: the London stone and the chalice that bore the heart of Saint George. Across from these objects was a cage, in which seven large ravens were perched, their frantic caws magically silenced, making them all the more piteous in their captivity. A woman stood beside the cage, stroking its bars as if to comfort the prisoners. She wore a blood-spattered gown of some ancient design, and her long dark hair was littered with bones and eyeballs. Another raven sat upon her shoulder. I recalled the name that Holmes had spoken in the comfort of our room. This hideous creature was the Morrigan, the chooser of the dead.

Swallowing my fear, I studied the point at the centre of the web. It consisted of a time-worn wooden chair in the Norman style, a seat that might well have predated even the manor around it. The golden threads of the web were woven through its back and sides, looking much like a set of glimmering bootlaces. Resting on the seat of the chair was a diminutive artefact. It was so tiny I could barely see it, yet it sparkled and gleamed, casting back an array of beautiful colours.

Titania's diadem. The one piece of the puzzle Holmes had never been quite able to fit together.

But where was Holmes? He had not spoken of taken on an invisibility spell, and except for the weird mechanism below, the room was essentially bare. I searched for him in the crannies and the shadows, but got no sign, not even a flicker of movement. At that moment, if I had possessed it still, I might well have sold my soul for one glimpse of Holmes' calm and self-assured profile, for my eyes had just fallen on the individuals whose evil work we had come to halt.

Marie Laveau, alias Lady Ariel Whitborne, stood to one side of the chair. She was tall and regal, but her face was the mottled green shade of a week-old corpse. She wore the bright colours and hooped skirt of the Southern states, the low bodice of her costume displaying the workings of graveyard corruption on her once-fine skin. She sported a turban as a crown, and regarded the entrance of Hypatia with arrogant amusement.

Beside her was her mate, her lover, her tool. The Baron Samedi was no longer dressed in his servant's attire, but as a fine gentleman with glossy boots, white gloves and a pearl tie tack. The black crepe band of his high silk hat trailed down his back. One further ghastly addition was the white paint on his face, drawn in the shape of a skull. It was no wonder than the ignorant peoples of the Caribbean islands had so eagerly worshipped and feared him. Just looking at him caused my knees to shake, and I felt myself unwillingly crouching on the catwalk, as if forced to acknowledge the majesty of death itself.

"The Lady Hypatia, you honour us by your presence," Laveau said, in a tone that still carried the strange accent of the city of her birth. "We would have called for you later in the evening."

"I know. I thought I would spare you the effort," she said, as if the two women were discussing a future luncheon or an impending meeting over tea. "I would prefer my beautiful Library not to be fouled with zombie gore."

"That was wise of you."

Hypatia acknowledged the compliment. Laveau waved her hand and the zombies retreated, moving to stand as silent guards at the door. "I see now why the marriage was necessary," Hypatia continued, "you needed the Whitborne

166

fortune. You required literally millions of pounds of gold to be melted down for your engine and to finance the alterations in the house, as well as the commissioning of that unfortunate goldsmith. He is dead, I presume."

"Dead and devoured by my pet in the fountain," Laveau said. "And the fact that you come to me only in the company of my guards suggests that you have equalled the score by doing away with Spring Heeled Jack."

"Gladly," Hypatia hissed. "You should thank me. He was only a distraction."

"He served his purpose," Laveau allowed, "which was my own necessary liberation, when the time was right."

"So you were merely absorbing the latent energies of the cemetery?" Hypatia inquired. Laveau laughed.

"I see you do more than guard your books, Madame, you actually read them. Yes, I was strengthening myself for my task by drawing to my body the last remnants of death magic, and when I completed my absorption Spring Heeled Jack was summoned to free me. He was also an efficient conveyor of the corpses from Highgate, from which I will build my undead army."

"And he was stupid enough to believe you would let him rule beside you, when you shatter the boundaries between the worlds," Hypatia concluded, with the amusement of a businessman admiring a rival's profitable deal. "Jack was

always a simpleton. But Morrigan, I expected better of you."
At that, Hypatia turned, directing her words to the crone who
stood beside the cage, leaning on a spear. "You are the elder,
and a true creature of Shadows, not a Halfling witch. You
should know that no plan to tilt the balance will ever succeed."

"I will be the harvester for my queen," she answered, in
a voice of rattling bones. "I will lead the armies of the dead,
and have first choice amid the fallen."

"At the cost of your own feathered children," Hypatia
reminded, gesturing at the cage. "I find your maternal instinct
sadly lacking."

"You think you are clever?" Laveau asked, striding
forward, closing the distance between she and Hypatia. "You
mock and bait, but if you know what we intend you also know
there is no hope for you to stop it."

"I could not agree with you more, foul queen," Hypatia
snapped. "The moment I did the calculations and extrapolated
the energy necessary to engage your magical device, I knew
there was no chance of escape. You need me. Without my
immortality—the only <u>human</u> immortality in existence---to fuel
it, even a machine made from the faith of centuries will run for
just a few short hours. That is barely the time required to cause
an earthquake, a flood, or a firestorm. Britain would suffer, but
the veil between the Sun and the Shadows would not be

permanently torn. The mortals would win. What you needed was the ultimate mechanical goal of *perpetual motion*."

"And we shall have it."

She spoke a word and Hypatia was flung backwards. The librarian collided with the chair, knocking the glittering crown to the floor. All around her, the golden threads came to life, twisting and writhing, binding her down to the seat.

Laveau retrieved the fallen symbol of royalty, cradling it in her palm. She glanced over her shoulder at the large Negro man, who had, throughout the dialogue, kept a respectful distance. "My darling, I will give you the honour of crowning her, if you wish it."

The Baron spoke in a low voice, hints of Africa in every vowel. "She is an unnatural thing, a human who lives forever. My power has no hold over her. I do not wish to touch her."

"But life is what we will use to bring about the death of the human worlds," Laveau predicted. "And once this key is fitted, the engine is turned on, and our work begins in earnest. We will put out the Sun."

I saw it all at once, the puzzle clicking together. The power of the relics would be sustained by the unending life that flowed from Hypatia's curse. The Fairy crown was the key, the focus that brought it to action. Once this terrible machine was activated, how could we ever turn it off?

I again looked around, now seeking not merely Holmes, but a weapon of some variety, anything that could bring a halt to the proceeding. My pistol seemed useless. I knew instinctively that none of the figures below would be harmed by its bullets. Perhaps there was a way of starting a fire, or bringing down the roof? I scurried to a corner where some ropes were coiled. As I reached for them my hand brushed against fabric.

I looked closer. It was a pile of garments, all of them familiar, including the great hound's-tooth cloak, the deerstalker cap, the boots with the pointed toes.

Hope abandoned me. Holmes was dead. They'd somehow discovered him and killed him, perhaps by some ghastly evaporation. He was nothing but dust within the wrinkles of this collection of fabric.

I nearly screamed. My mind turned red with fury.

And then I heard the great cawing of a raven. I spun and looked over the railing.

Laveau had begun to chant as a prelude to placing the diadem on Hypatia's brow. Her words now ceased. She scowled at the Morrigan, as if displeased by the interruption, like an opera diva hearing an orchestra strike a sour note. The raven that had perched on the Morrigan's shoulder took wing, circling above the voodoo queen and the infernal device made of gold and ancient artefacts. Then, before anyone could raise

170

a hand, it swooped at Baron Samedi's face. He shouted and struck at the bird, but the raven had already plucked free the cotton wads that plugged his nostrils.

Laveau's scream rang against the walls. Great buckets of blood gushed from the loa's nose. He swatted at his face, jerking and reeling. Laveau dropped the Fae crown and rushed to him, but already vast streams of blood, now mixed with brains, were cascading to the floor. He fell writhing inside the pool of his own corruption, and as I watched in wonder, he began to shrink. With every second his body was drawn tighter and tighter, even as Laveau keened and sobbed helplessly. At last he was no more than a brittle doll, a tiny figure sodden in the filth that his body had ejected.

Laveau rose, stepping away from the creature that had once been her mate. She glared at the Morrigan, who likewise stared at the miniaturized body as if startled and baffled by the violent turn of events.

"You bitch!" Laveau shrieked. "You traitor!"

"It was not my doing!" the ancient crone protested.

"How can you say that? Was it not your own familiar who un-worked him?"

"I do not understand, I---"

Laveau's hands began to glow. The Morrigan raised her spear. I spared a glance at Hypatia, saw her draw back within her bonds, her expression one of complete shock. She had planned her entrance, but not this unlikely turn.

A fireball shot from Laveau's fingertips. The Morrigan countered, wielding her spear like a cricket bat. The ball of flames was knocked away, but much to my misfortune, it ricocheted up and struck the catwalk. The entire structure began to melt. I hurried for the ladder, feeling it heating up beneath my fingertips. It gave way only seconds before I could leap free. I hit the floor, covering my head as blistering hot metal spewed around me.

Lifting up cautiously, I saw that the women were still duelling, Marie Laveau hurling alternating spheres of fire and ice at her rival. The Morrigan sought an advantage, no doubt hoping to impale the American witch with her spear. But Laveau was faster and more powerful. A blue globe struck the Morrigan squarely in her chest, and she turned instantly into a figure made of snow, a sculpture that twinkled and sparkled like a child's innocent dream.

Laveau hissed a single word, and the creature of Shadows who had once roamed Britain's ancient battlefields, had been worshipped with bowls of blood, melted into a pathetic puddle.

Laveau turned. Her eyes fastened on me. I was not sure how, but with another word I was suddenly being dragged before her. Invisible hands forced me to my knees, holding me down.

"A man who wishes to remain invisible should not be foolish enough to allow himself to be covered in ashes," Laveau said, snatching the ring from my finger. "So this is the famous Doctor Watson, the lackey, the chronicler, the dog who cowers before his master's whip. Tell me, where is that Half-Fae bastard that you worship?"

"You killed him," I snarled. I had suddenly forgotten life and death and fear. All I could see was the empty pile of clothing that had represented such a noble and brave man. "You destroyed him!"

"Did I now?" Laveau asked, taking several steps back from me. "If so, then it will be all the easier to kill you."

I lifted my head, determined to meet her fatal spell like a man and a British soldier.

Much to my astonishment, the great raven that had attacked Baron Samedi, only to be ignored in the fray of the witches' duel, landed on the floor between myself and my executioner. Before I could draw breath, the bird rose skyward again, its form changing shape. Its wings became arms, its talons legs. Feathers flowed into new dimensions and textures. Its body expanded to a height of some six feet, with broad shoulders and long limbs—human limbs covered in skin.

173

Laveau now confronted a nude male body wearing a familiar face.

Chapter Twenty-two

"Holmes!"

I had never been happier to see anyone in my life, even if in a very total state of undress. Laveau stepped back and sideways, her lips twisting into a snarl.

"You would sink to such taboos?" Laveau snarled. "Make yourself an animal?"

"A bird, to be precise. I have always found the experience of becoming a *hamingja* to be exhilarating and liberating. It is also a useful form for surveillance."

"I was warned about you," Laveau hissed. I heard Holmes chuckle, as if nothing could or would intimidate him.

"Wicked people always are," he said, and rolled out his arms, the gesture of an actor offering a bow. At that moment, his skin was covered with garments spun of shadow, so that he appeared to be wearing a fitted suit of deepest mourning. He eased backward and waggled the fingers of his right hand. Suddenly I was free of Laveau's invisible grip. "I can offer you a choice, Marie Laveau," Holmes announced. "An honest death this time, a chance for absolution. There is a higher Power than even we wield, and it might yet forgive you all your sins."

She sneered. "I care nothing for your mercy."

"Then you will face my wrath."

She flung her right arm forward; Holmes' left hand shot out, palm open. Something like a great shield covered us, so that the heat Laveau projected roiled around it. Holmes twisted, shouting to me.

"Release Hypatia and run!"

"But the machine---"

"It is useless without her. GO!"

I scrambled to my feet. Holmes brought his other hand up and the room was abruptly plunged into near total darkness. I felt my way along, my hands clasping a single golden thread, following it to the chair where Hypatia was imprisoned. Laveau shrieked. The overheated air was filled with her curses and what sounded like the crashing of great cymbals. I risked a glimpse back, saw the shadows of witch and wizard pounding one another, flinging magical energy that, for all I knew, could kill a mortal at the slightest touch. Then I perceived another threat, the zombie guards lurching away from the door. They slowly made their way toward us, jabbering and croaking, arms extended.

Darkness descended, scarlet lights flared, darkness reclaimed the room. The sharp, flickering contrast was maddening. I staggered with every other step.

"Hypatia!"

My hand closed around one of hers. In a lightning strobe I saw that she was terrified. Even in that awful place, my instinct was to comfort her.

"I'll free you."

"Doctor, you can't! You're human, you can't work this magic! You don't know the words."

I tugged at the bonds. By all rights, the gold was thin in places and I should have been capable of bending or breaking it. Yet I could not, and the lady remained a prisoner.

I turned back. Holmes had no time to assist me. His own battle was raging, he was like a prize-fighter taking blow after blow in hopes of dancing closer, delivering some knockout punch. I would have to solve this riddle on my own.

The zombies were drawing closer, awkwardly making their way through the woven threads of the golden web. They would fall, but doggedly rise again, heedless of loosing bit of their bodies as they moved.

I looked around and saw the tiny Fae diadem where it had been dropped on the floor. I snatched it up, showed it to Hypatia.

"Will it give me the knowledge of magic?" I demanded, thinking of all the stories I had heard as a lad, of boys who donned thinking caps and suddenly outsmarted their tutors. Hypatia drew back, her breath rasping.

"Yes, but---no, Doctor, don't! Don't!"

She had said the only word I needed to hear, which was 'yes.' I clapped the crown to my own head.

In one heartbeat, my mind was opened. I saw, I thought, I knew in ways that would never have been possible without supernatural aid. For the briefest of moments, I was working all puzzles, solving all crimes, revealing all mysteries. It is impossible to write in mere words what I experienced, how in that crystalline instant I simply became aware of all of my brain, instead of the tiniest portion that humans are able to use. The best way I can describe it is to say that, for just a brief moment in time, I possessed a mind equal to Holmes'.

The pain was unbearable. I emitted an agonized scream.

And then duty recalled me. I knew the words that would unlock the spells, force the golden thread to release Hypatia. I whispered them without conscious effort, as if they were the words of nursery rhymes I had learned in the cradle. The cords shot free and Hypatia pushed from the chair. She slapped me, hard.

The crown fell from my head. I sank to the floor in relief.

"Oh, my brave Doctor," Hypatia sighed, struggling to pull me up, "another second and it would have killed you!"

There was a loud grunt. A corrupted arm shot around Hypatia's throat, towing her backwards. I fought to rise, but a bare foot, made of nothing but jagged bones, kicked me down. It aimed again, striving to stab me with a shattered heel. I caught an exposed femur, twisted, and threw the monster off balance.

"Doctor!"

Hypatia's cry was strangled short. I looked up just as she managed to free her long knife from her belt, tossing it toward me. The zombie's fingers tightened on her throat, faster than I could move.

There was an audible snap. The lady's neck was broken. Hypatia crumpled lifeless in the zombie's arms.

I rose, taking up Hypatia's weapon. The zombie snarled at me, and for just a moment I was stuck numb with horror.

I knew the face, the man. Stamford, the dresser, the very youth who had introduced me to Holmes. I had attended his funeral only the year before, when he had been cut down by cancer in the prime of his life.

I raised the machete and struck him a blow across the scalp. He staggered, releasing his victim. I pushed on, brought the blade down again and removed his head.

His soul was gone, and no further evil would use his flesh.

The zombie who had attacked me crouched on broken knees. He propelled himself toward Hypatia, mouth open, as if determined to feast on her. Without thought, I swung my blade, sliced off his head and sent him into eternity. I pulled Hypatia into my arms, mourning her, knowing from the bubble of blood on her lips and the coldness of her face, she was surely beyond my aid.

She started abruptly, and drew breath again, blinking at my undoubtedly astonished face.

"Why do men never believe me?" she posed, lifting a slender finger to tap against my moustache. "We must help Holmes," she reminded. I nodded eagerly, and we stood together, hand in hand.

The battle did not seem to be going in Holmes' favour. He had fallen to his knees, his face bathed in sweat. I started forward, but Hypatia held me back.

"There is only one thing Laveau fears. Fire from the world of the Sun, not the Shadows-fire that she casts."

I nodded my understanding. I took the brandy flask, splashed a generous dollop over the bodies of the zombies. Hypatia removed her jacket, dipping it in the splattering alcohol. I found a match in my pocket and struck it, dropping it onto the fuel. Greedy combustion licked over the bodies and Hypatia's attire. She grabbed the edge of her coat and hurried to one side of the room, to ignite the ancient walls. I likewise sought a method of furthering the conflagration. I literally stumbled over Holmes' clothes, where they had fallen from the catwalk. I was poised to strike a second match when I recalled an essential item within Holmes' discarded coat. I fished out the silver cigarette case and slid it into my own pocket, then fired the clothes and flung them to the opposite wall.

The fire leapt and roared, flames shooting up into the rafters like a million eager imps. The centuries' old structure was perfect kindling. Laveau shrieked, for a moment losing her focus, even as I heard Holmes shout "good show!" He aimed a bolt of blue lightning at the voodoo queen, but she dropped and the force struck the eastern wall, blasting an opening to the true night.

"Come on!" Hypatia urged, for the intensity of the heat was scorching my skin, and beams were dropping all around us. I started to follow, but at that moment I saw something that stopped my heart.

As Laveau's palms hit the floor a sheet of ice sprang from them. Holmes was advancing, no doubt to deliver the fatal strike, but he slipped. I expected him to spring back to his feet, but he failed to rally. His body was limp; perhaps he had been knocked unconscious. The witch gave a shout of triumph and skidded toward him, pulling a dagger from her voluminous skirts. Holmes' own words were in my head---*I am as mortal as you are*.

He could be killed in a very ordinary fashion.

I was about to watch him die.

Chapter Twenty-three

My hands flew to the cigarette case. I flicked it open and prayed that I was right, that my instinct had not failed me.

"Save him," I ordered.

The golden bee buzzed from the case and flew as straight and true as any arrow. It attacked the witch, darting directly into her eyes. She screamed and batted at it. Her cries roused Holmes from his stupor.

He seized the dagger she had dropped and drove it hard into the base of her throat.

For an instant they were frozen in that pose. Laveau's eyes glared at him. Her teeth were exposed like that of a charging lioness. Then she shuddered, gave a low moan, and tumbled backward. Holmes pulled himself over her, the way a man might rest above a lover. Hypatia shoved me sideways.

"Holmes, no!" she shouted, desperate to be heard over the crackling and snapping of the burning wood. "You do not want this!"

Holmes turned to look at Hypatia, and I saw that his eyes were glowing red. A strange energy suddenly burst from him, causing every hair on my head to rise and the floorboards beneath me to vibrate.

"What is happening?" I pleaded.

"Wizards can claim the power of those they best in duels," Hypatia answered, her words trembling. "Holmes, NO!

You must not take her energy. With it comes her evil. Think what she was capable of!"

I understood at last what Holmes had meant by so many of his enigmatic statements. He had always walked a fine line between doing good and doing as he pleased. More than once he had played judge and jury. Whenever it suited his purposes, he had broken the law without the least sign of hesitation or remorse. I saw in a flash all the temptations he faced, and knew that should he suck down the departing power of this, the greatest of all American witches, he would be beyond the ability of any force to control him. Sun and Shadows, he could rule them all.

He knew it, too. I could see it on his features, in the ugly curve of his smile. It gave him the appearance of a predatory beast about to feast on its kill.

"Holmes," I said, moving forward like a man propelled by a dream. "This is the Reichenbach from which you can not escape!" I was flooded with memories of that terrible time when I thought Holmes dead. I knew should he take on Laveau's powers there would be nothing that could save him. Even if he never died, he would surely lose his soul and we would be bound to the Void together. "Please, old friend," I begged, "step away from that dark chasm."

I held my hand out to him. He studied me, all the magical powers of both worlds at war in his features. Then, with the desperation of a drowning man seizing a lifeline, he grabbed my fingers. I pulled him to my side, holding him tightly.

Laveau's mouth sagged open. A purple miasma curled upward from her sagging jaw.

Perhaps it was only a trick of the light, but I would be prepared to swear that I saw a certain effrontery at defeat, an anger in the final closing of that terrible woman's eyes, as if cheated of a revenge from beyond the grave.

"We must go," Holmes said.

"The relics," I shouted, as he began to pull me along after him, Hypatia flanking us. "What about them?"

Holmes halted, studying the shattered, melted remains of the great machine. Hypatia tilted her head.

"Five pounds says you can't do it, you are far too exhausted."

He arched a dark brow. "Ten says that I can."

I had no idea what either Hypatia or Holmes meant. My friend flung his hands out, whispered a final, ragged incantation.

The London Stone, the Heart of Saint George, Titania's crown and the cage filled with ravens all vanished with a loud pop, simply disappearing as if sucked into some unseen vortex. My friend's eyes rolled back and he dropped senseless to the floor.

"Holmes!" I yelped.

"Grab his arm, Doctor!" Hypatia favoured me with a saucy wink, "I knew that a banishment spell would do him in. He'll be less fuss and bother this way, trust me. And all the relics have been sent home; it will be as if they had never been away."

Together, we dragged Holmes a safe distance from the house. As the flames shot skyward I heard the clanging of fire engine bells in the distance. I was relieved to see two other figures stumbling about on the lawn. Sir James and Robert stared at the inferno in wonder, arms around each other. At Hypatia's insistence, we kept away from them, remaining cloaked by the deep shadows of the great elms.

Much to my astonishment, the enchanted bee appeared in a twinkle of light and landed on Holmes' shoulder, creeping closer and nuzzling his jaw like a devoted hound.

Some two hours passed before Holmes woke up. His first action was to consider his tutor with a sour expression on his soot-blackened face. "You tricked me," he accused.

"You should learn to resist a wager," she chided. In the time we had sat hidden from the Whitbornes and the fire-fighters, Hypatia had told me many things about Holmes. I now had a wealth of embarrassing stories of childhood experiments gone awry or youthful mysteries that were solved only to cause civil wars among the Fae. I grasped more fully why Holmes lived as an outcast to the Shadows. I also understood why he was tempted by Laveau's power, which would have given him mastery over the very world he had rejected.

I could tell from the look Holmes turned on me that he knew exactly what Hypatia had been doing while he was senseless. He emitted a low groan and wiped his hands over his face.

"There will be no mocking you now, will there, Watson?"

"Not without consequences, Holmes." I gestured toward the manor. The firemen had miraculously prevented the blaze from spreading. "What about the corpses in the eastern wing of the property? Surely they will be discovered and the innocent Whitbornes arrested."

Holmes sat up, giving a thoughtful nod. "Mycroft has failed to tow his own tremendous weight in this matter. I will have him make arrangements through the Home Office. The affair will be quietly settled, and the bodies returned to consecrated ground." He looked to Hypatia. "You took a foolish risk."

"I merely followed the same path of logic you did and came to the identical conclusion," she countered proudly. "They would have come for me anyway. What is your maxim about the element of surprise? I had it against them, so I would have been a fool not to use it."

"And you truly can not die?" I asked, expecting---to be honest---another slap for my curiosity, which she might take as impudence.

"Doctor, you continue to see, but not observe," Hypatia laughed. "I can die, over and over again, but I can not <u>stay</u> dead; that is why they sought me as the energy for their awful machine. Had they succeeded in their plan I would have spent an eternity in agony, dying instantly only to be instantly reborn." She rose and dusted off her jodhpurs. "I think it is time I went back to my Library, where the greatest terror is dust or the occasional bookworm."

Chapter Twenty-four

I had barely touched my coffee the following morning when Holmes strode into the room like a conquering hero, waving a vial like a sabre.

"She was true to her word, Watson---though the High Queen did wish to know what manner of rogue had so rudely dented her diadem."

I swallowed nervously. "Surely you did not tell her the truth."

"I blamed it all on Marie Laveau. There are many among the realms of both Sun and Shadows who will rest easier, knowing that she has finally been dispatched. Ah, and there is the door. One minute if you please."

He handed me the glass vial. I stared at it, marvelling at the twinkling blue vapours within. I had always envisioned a soul as a spirit or ghost, not a working of the light. The thought that I held my own soul in my hand was as humbling as it was awe-inspiring.

"Just as I had hoped, Watson," Holmes said, re-entering and placing a shoe box sized parcel on the table beside my breakfast. "A fireman fished this from the ruins. My brother's silent agents retrieved it, and now he forwards it along to me."

"But I thought you sent all the relics to their proper destinations with the banishment spell?"

"I did. This is no relic. It is an adversary."

I rose from the table in a rush, nearly---much to my embarrassment---toppling my own soul in the process. Holmes directed me to place the glass vial on the safety of his chemistry table. I returned just as he finished undoing the package.

"Watson, say hello again to Baron Samedi."

I sucked in a sharp breath. A blackened, withered doll lay at the bottom of the box. White eyes bulged, sharp teeth grimaced. The body was still dressed in finery, right down to tiny white funeral gloves. It seemed rigid, a form carved from wood, but it radiated something evil and repulsive. Even though it looked lifeless, I sensed an active intelligence, and an awful patience. This thing was bidding its time to strike again.

"When, in the guise of a raven, I removed his nostril plugs, he lost the gathered power of his own faithful worshippers," Holmes explained. "But he is a loa of death itself, a dark spirit, and therefore can not be killed with any finality. Nor would we want to, for that might affect the balance between the worlds. Can you imagine a world in which no one died?"

"One would think it would be wonderful."

"Only until all the crops were consumed by hungry, immortal mouths and all the houses filled. Imagine the press of humanity growing every greater by the moment, crawling over

189

each other like ants in a mound or overrun like oysters on the bottom of the sea. No, Watson, even Baron Samedi has his place. Death is as important as life."

"So what will you do with him?"

Holmes closed the box. It made me think of a coffin lid coming down for the final time. "Tonight I will open another tunnel through the Shadows and take him back to Haiti. His followers there will know how to revive him. With any luck, the unpleasantness of his little foray onto English soil will convince him not to take any more powerful witches as lovers."

"May I accompany you?" I asked eagerly. "I have never been to the Caribbean."

He turned, and the look he gave me was a sad one. "Watson...there is something I must tell you."

"Yes, Holmes?"

"When you reabsorb your soul---an act that you must perform, moments from now---it is very likely you will forget everything that has happened in the last few days."

"Why?" I asked, feeling a wave of disappointment sweep over me.

"Innocent mortals were never meant to know the secrets of the Shadows, Watson. Your knowledge is dangerous, to you and those around you."

"But Holmes, think how I could help. I could be of service to you!"

He nodded, and a tinge of shame crept onto his cheeks. "I realize that, Watson. And were the choice my own, I would not hesitate to keep you apprised. But it is simply a factor of the magic that is your human essence."

"But I thought human possessed no magic!"

Holmes shook his head, and once more I felt like a pupil who had disappointed his teacher. "All humans have some magic within them. Otherwise, witches such as Laveau could not exist, nor would Hypatia's body have embraced such an unusual curse. Your magic will dictate whether your mind and body can bear the strain."

"So there is a chance I might remember?"

"A very slim one, Watson. It has happened a few times, but it is most rare."

I considered his words, and looked back to the vial that held my soul. I had no wish to prolong its absence from me. After all, no man knows the hour when his reckoning with the Almighty is due.

"Holmes," I said, my mouth dry as powder, "what was the chance that young Stamford, God rest his soul, would have introduced me to you in the chemical laboratory at St. Barts? If there ever was an unlikely, magical thing, it is our friendship, not the juxtaposition of Sun and Shadows."

"Well said, Watson."

"But still...should this prove to be my final hour of memory, my last awareness of who and what you really are, then there is something I must complete."

****

And so this ink is spilled across the blank page. I have written the story that must never be told. It is a tale for which the world is not prepared, a narrative that, if I were to read it later on, I would deny authoring

But it is the truth. I swear it.

In mere moments I will press the vial to my lips and, in one breath, recall my soul. Holmes warns me that my mind will cloud, and that all will be forgotten. If so, so be it. I can only pray it will not happen. I will regret the loss of those fine moments, that shining victory we shared.

Most of all, my dear Hypatia, I will regret that I will never have known you. Perhaps even now you are reading these lines, deep within the confines of your most unusual library. In them, I keep my promise to you, to provide you with a complete recounting of our case. What you do with this memoir, I leave to your discretion. You may show it to the world, or hide it deep within that arcane labyrinth. I wish I had been more poetic in my prose, my dear lady. It is obvious to me that Holmes loves you as a mentor and teacher; had I been given time, I would have done my best to have loved you as more.

The story is done. Perhaps I will remember. Perhaps I will forget.

The sunlight is fading. Now the shadows fall.

Also from MX Publishing:

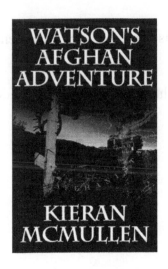

Kieran McMullen

Watson's Afghan Adventure

www.mxpublishing.co.uk

Also from MX Publishing:

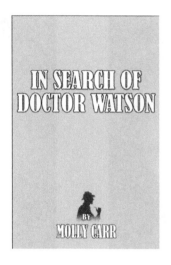

Molly Carr

In Search of Dr.Watson – A Sherlockian Investigation

The definitive biography of Dr.Watson

www.mxpublishing.co.uk

Molly Carr

The Sign of Fear
And
A Study In Crimson

The first two adventures of Mrs. Watson with a supporting cast including Sherlock Holmes, Dr. Watson and Moriarty

www.mxpublishing.co.uk

Also from MX Publishing:

John H Watson

Edited by Tony Reynolds

**The recent decease of one of the descendents of Dr. Watson
has brought to light his personal papers. These include a
number of stories that Dr. Watson suppressed at the time
for various reasons. As all involved are long dead, the
inheritor has agreed to the publication of a set of eight of
the most interesting adventures.**

www.mxpublishing.co.uk

Also from MX Publishing:

Kieron Freeburn

The Official Papers Into The Matter Known As The Hound of the Baskervilles (DCC/1435/89 refers)

The original police papers from the Hound of The Baskervilles case discovered by real-life 'Sherlock Holmes', former Metropolitan Police detective Kieron Freeburn.

www.mxpublishing.co.uk

Also from MX Publishing:

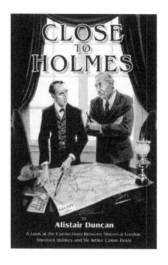

Alistair Duncan

Close To Holmes

A Look at the Connections Between Historical London, Sherlock Holmes and Sir Arthur Conan Doyle

www.mxpublishing.co.uk

Also from MX Publishing:

Alistair Duncan

Eliminate the Impossible

An Examination of the World of Sherlock Holmes on Page and Screen

www.mxpublishing.co.uk

Also from MX Publishing:

Alistair Duncan

The Norwood Author

**Arthur Conan Doyle
and the Norwood Years (1891 - 1894)**

www.mxpublishing.co.uk

Also from MX Publishing:

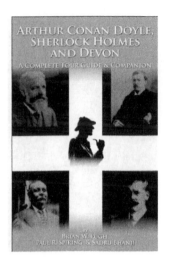

Brian W. Pugh and Paul R. Spiring

Arthur Conan Doyle, Sherlock Holmes and Devon

A Complete Tour Guide and Companion

www.mxpublishing.co.uk

Also from MX Publishing:

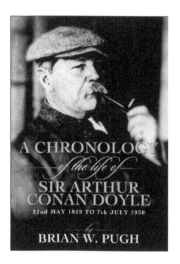

Brian W. Pugh

A Chronology of The Life Of Sir Arthur Conan Doyle

A Detailed Account Of The Life And Times Of The Creator Of Sherlock Holmes

www.mxpublishing.co.uk

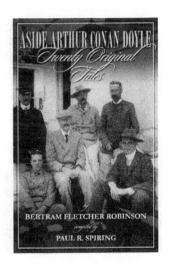

Paul R. Spiring

Aside Arthur Conan Doyle

Twenty Original Tales By Bertram Fletcher Robinson

www.mxpublishing.co.uk

Lightning Source UK Ltd.
Milton Keynes UK
UKOW06f2218171115

262941UK00001B/5/P